The Moon Rock Heist

Betty Harman
and
Nancy Meador

EAKIN PRESS ☆ Austin, Texas

FIRST EDITION

Copyright © 1988
By Betty Harman and Nancy Meador

Published in the United States of America
By Eakin Press, P.O. Box 23069, Austin, Texas 78735

ISBN 0-89015-667-0

Library of Congress Cataloging-in-Publication Data

Harman, Betty, 1932–
    The moon rock heist / by Betty Harman and Nancy Meador.
        p.   cm.
    Summary: Joseph and his Vietnamese American friend Huy investigate the disappearance of a moon rock loaned by NASA to their high school in Galveston Bay.
    ISBN 0-89015-667-0 : $9.95
    [1. Mystery and detective stories. 2. Vietnamese Americans — Fiction. 3. Friendship — Fiction. 4. Texas — Fiction.] I. Meador, Nancy, 1922– II. Title.
PZ7.H22668Mo   1988
[Fic] — dc19   88-16274
                                                                        CIP
                                                                        AC

To our rock-hound friend, Fay,
who showed us the way to the moon rocks.

Preface

Lunar samples, more popularly known as "moon rocks," belong to all of us. Since the Apollo missions were paid for by the American taxpayers, the samples belong to the American people.

Gathered by Apollo astronauts on six different landings on the moon, the collection of nearly 900 pounds of material is now housed at the Johnson Space Center in Houston, Texas. It is composed of more than 2,000 separate samples.

Specimens from this collection are available to private citizens simply by filling out a few easy forms and watching an instructional filmstrip. At any given time, moon rocks can be found in the hands of scientists, professors, schoolteachers, and students all over the world.

In this fictional adventure, a moon rock gets into the hands of the wrong people . . .

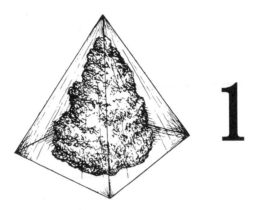

1

Joseph Boyd rolled the flat, round film can into its place on the slanted library shelf. He turned it so that the outside call number could be seen. Upside down! One would think that at least half the time the number would be right-side-up, but Joseph felt sure this fifty-fifty ratio did not apply to shelving library material. He pulled the can out, turned it over, and slipped it back into its place just as the bell announced the end of the school day. Almost immediately, he heard locker doors slamming and a swell of student voices in the corridor on the other side of the wall.

Joseph felt grateful that he had this library job his freshman year in high school. He loved to read. Besides, he knew that he was too small and too undisciplined to ever be outstanding in athletics. He did enjoy swimming and had, on his first try, made the school swim team. In water everything came naturally and easily to him. At first he had dreaded competition; but after several successful meets, his self-confidence had grown. In spite of this, Joseph still considered himself a spectator, a dreamer, and a planner. And right now, his plans included

1

nothing more than finishing this year of school and spending the summer exploring the beach with his dog, Lonesome, and his best friend, Huy. Huy, also fourteen, worked in the library with him.

Huy was a loner. His dark hair and Oriental eyes gave him a look of sadness, but Joseph knew that in spite of his friend's reserve, he was intelligent and fun-loving.

Joseph looked at him now and laughed. Poor Huy was in the throes of trying to fold up a stubborn projection screen. The portable screen had earned the nickname of "Jezebel" by the teachers and staff alike. Joseph's eyes glittered with anticipation as he watched the dual gymnastic routine of the screen and Huy. Everyone knew that the grooves at the bottom and a red lever held the legs up and in place for screen storage. And nearly everyone knew that a second red button regulated the height of the screen with a post that slid up and down and that a lever held the rolled-up screen in place. Everyone seemed to know these things except Huy.

Huy struggled with the post that held the screen in place since the rolled screen was already producing a windmill effect. Then, by accident, he pressed the middle red button and *down* slammed the post. The impact jarred loose the leg lever and the legs triangled out full span. He was back where he started. Joseph held his sides with laughter. Huy stared steely black darts at Joseph.

"You make a lot of noise for such a little fellow."

"I may be a little fellow, but I am smarter than you are," Joseph said as he wiped tears from his eyes.

"What makes you so smart?"

"You didn't see me take on Old Jezebel, did you?"

"Well, I'm smarter now," grumbled Huy. "This old girl and I are through."

"Next time, we'll both attack her. Surely she can't beat us both. Actually, with what we know about her habits, we could use her as a secret weapon."

They heard a loud crack.

2

"What was that?" Huy asked.

"I don't know — maybe your screen was just getting in the last word."

"No, I didn't mean that cracking sound . . . that came from outside. Listen."

The halls were quieter now.

"It sounds like Miss Duncan. She is calling for help!"

Both boys rushed out the door of the A-V room and dashed across the entire length of the library reading room before they reached the librarian's office. There, the cries for help were distinctly audible.

Miss Duncan was on her knees on the floor. Only her feet and legs could be seen. Her head and upper body were stuffed inside a blue duffel bag, which was drawn and tied tightly around her thighs.

"Miss Duncan," Joseph cried, "are you all right?"

"Is that you, Joseph?" Her voice sounded muffled. "Please, help me get out of this thing."

"Yes, ma'am. Huy is with me. Just be still and let us get this rope untied."

"Are you hurt?" asked Huy, already beginning to work at the knotted rope. "This is a hard square knot. It may take me a minute to loosen it."

"No, I think I am all right. Maybe one of you should call the main office. Try to get Mr. Greyson if you can and ask him to come down here."

Joseph picked up the phone, which was almost hidden under books and papers piled on the librarian's desk. He dialed the office extension.

As he waited for an answer, he noticed the small metal container which held the flat lucite disk of rocks and soil samples gathered from the moon by the Apollo astronauts. For a moment his mind froze. Where was the large pyramid-shaped case that held the big rock? And where was the metal container that Miss Duncan used to transport the rock to the police station for overnight storage? His eyes searched the crowded desk, the floor, the office shelves, and a flat book truck near the desk.

3

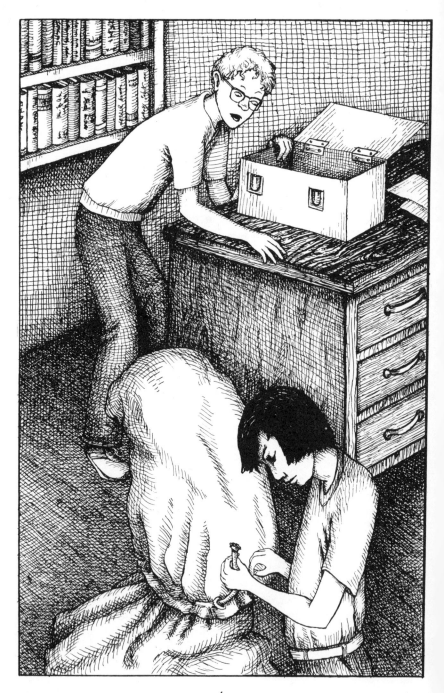

A voice on the telephone jarred him back to the immediate emergency. He explained what had happened to Miss Duncan and was assured that the principal would be reached and sent right down.

"Thank you," he said weakly and hung up. "Miss Duncan ..." He hesitated, swallowed, and then continued, "Did you know that the big moon rock is not here?"

He heard a gasp from inside the bag.

"Oh, no! So that is what they were after. Oh, Huy, can you hurry, please?"

"Just a minute," Huy answered. "I almost have it now."

The knot was loose enough now to pull one of the rope ends through. Huy pulled it out and began loosening the drawstring around the librarian's thighs. This accomplished, he was able to pull the duffel bag from over her head.

"Oh, thank you, Huy," she said rising to her feet by holding on to the edge of the desk. Her usually neat auburn hair was completely disheveled. Long strands had worked loose from the French roll she wore and now hung below her shoulders. Joseph was amazed at the little-girl look this gave her as she turned her frightened green eyes toward him.

"Are you sure, Joseph? Is it really gone?"

Joseph pointed to the smaller case.

"I had just finished putting in the small disk. The large rock was here on the desk. What could anyone want with it? What could anyone do with it after they had stolen it?"

"Stolen what?" The question came from the doorway. It was the principal, Mr. Greyson. "Miss Duncan, what has happened? Are you hurt? You look ill. Perhaps you should sit down. Tell me what has been stolen."

Miss Duncan gave a hollow laugh. "May we take it one question at a time?" she asked. "I am still just a little shaken."

"Of course, of course, I'm sorry. Here, sit down, sit

5

down." Mr. Greyson had a habit of repeating words when he was nervous. This was particularly true when he spoke over the intercom or in assembly programs.

Miss Duncan went to the chair behind her desk and sat.

"It's the moon rock. I'm afraid I am in big trouble."

"The moon rock? How could such a thing happen?" He turned to Joseph and Huy. "What were you two boys doing in this office?"

"We weren't, sir. We were in the A-V room," Joseph said. "We came when we heard her calling for help."

"Did you see anything? Anything? Anyone leaving the office? Anyone in the library? Anyone?" He was looking at Huy.

"No, sir." Huy shook his head.

The principal turned to Miss Duncan. "How about you? Surely you saw who attacked you?"

Miss Duncan pointed at the duffel bag and shook her head.

"No. They slipped up behind me and pulled that over my head. I couldn't see anything."

"Oh, my . . . Oh, my! I had better call the police." Mr. Greyson started toward the telephone.

"No," Miss Duncan said, "you need to call the National Aeronautics and Space Administration. They warned us that if anything happened to the specimens that it would be investigated by the FBI."

"The FBI? Good heavens, Miss Duncan! What have you gotten us into? How much was that rock worth? And why did you take it into your head to borrow it anyway? How valuable is it?"

"It is considered a priceless national treasure," Miss Duncan said calmly. "And I borrowed it for our display to commemorate the *Challenger* crew that perished. You gave your written permission for me to do so." Miss Duncan began to recover some of her usual composure and poise. As she talked, she pulled hair pins from the back of her head, letting the rest of her thick hair fall down her back. Now she gathered the entire mass together in her left hand and with a few deft motions twisted it into a long coil and pinned it back into a French roll.

"Yes, yes, Miss Duncan, I am sure that I did. Don't get upset. Do you have the number to call at NASA?"

"Yes." She pulled a card from her top desk drawer and handed it to the principal.

"What shall I tell them?" Mr. Greyson asked. "What were you doing with the rock at the time?"

"I was packing it in its case," she explained, "to take it to the police station. One of the requirements for checking the specimen out is to never leave it unattended, except when it is in the safe." She turned to the boys.

"Thank you, Joseph. Thank you, Huy. You boys were very helpful. There is nothing else you can do now. Why don't you go on home?"

Huy stepped forward and bowed slightly. "I am very happy that you were not hurt," he said. "May we get you anything before we go?"

Miss Duncan smiled. "No, thank you. That is very sweet, but I am fine."

Joseph got his jacket from the coat rack in the corner and put it on. Huy came toward the rack with a puzzled expression on his face.

"My coat is not here." He looked at Joseph. "I put it right here when we came in last period."

"Yeah, I remember," Joseph said. "We hung them up together before we started clearing tables in the reading room."

"Are you sure?" the principal broke in. "Do you think whoever took the rock might have taken your coat?"

"I don't know." Huy hesitated. "Could they have taken it to conceal the rock?"

"You may be right," the principal agreed. "I had better get that call in to NASA. You boys go home." He began dialing.

Joseph and Huy waved quietly to Miss Duncan and left the office.

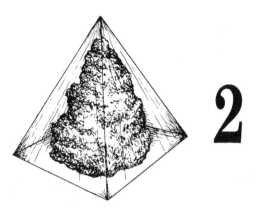

2

"What do you think?" Joseph asked as they stood in the hall outside the library door.

"I don't know," Huy answered. "What should we do now? Mr. Greyson surely didn't want us to hang around here."

"No, he made that clear. I want to talk to Mother. She is already at the hospital. She is working the three-to-eleven shift today. Do you want to go over there with me, or do you need to go home?"

Huy hesitated a moment, then shook his head. "I had better go home. Father is cleaning and painting the boat for the Blessing of the Fleet next Sunday. He will expect me to help. I suppose I should tell my father about this too. After you talk with your mother, can you come down? Maybe we can go out on the jetty and talk. Besides, Lonesome will want to see you."

"Right." Joseph smiled. "Sure, I'll be there as soon as I can."

Lonesome was a stray dog which Joseph had found and claimed. He had stumbled upon him last September when he cut across a drainage ditch at the side of the

8

school campus. He would not have seen the dog at all had not the tall grass at the end of the concrete culvert been mashed flat. A slight movement had caught Joseph's eye. A black head with ears bent forward at the tips and large black eyes had peered inquiringly from the end of the pipe. The thump of a tail wagging timidly had echoed from within the culvert.

Joseph had squatted down and looked inside. The pup looked to be mostly of the border collie breed, although it was hard to tell. At the time, he was half-starved and dirty. Mange had claimed several large spots of his long, curly, black coat. Ticks, fleas, and dirt had matted and dulled the rest. It had taken several weeks of bathing with a solution to cure the mange and several sacks of good dog food to turn him into the healthy, shining dog that he was now.

Since Joseph lived in an apartment complex which did not allow pets, Huy, with the permission of his father, had offered to keep Lonesome on his boat. Many of the shrimpers kept dogs on board at night. They acted as guards and sentinels to alert the owners if anyone approached the boat. This was particularly important for the Vietnamese owners. Vandalism and even more serious damage was not uncommon at night. The arrangement had worked out well. Lonesome had a good home, and Joseph and Huy had become even closer friends since they shared in the care and joy of having a dog together.

The hospital was almost a mile from the school, so Joseph decided to go by the apartment first and pick up his bicycle. He had gotten out of the habit of riding his bicycle to school since he went home with Huy almost every afternoon. Somehow, he hated to do anything that drew attention to the fact that he had things that Huy didn't have — not that it would have made any difference to their friendship. Huy accepted life as it was. Joseph knew that Huy still had childhood memories of unhappier times, with the horrors of war and escape from his own country.

9

As he neared the hospital, Joseph's thoughts changed to his mother. He knew that she, too, remembered unhappier times. Joseph had been too young to remember when his father had left them, but he did recall the years they lived with his grandparents while his mother went to school to become a nurse. He remembered the argument between her and his grandparents. His grandmother and grandfather had said some terrible things about his father, but his mother would still never say anything bad about him. She had told Joseph only about the pleasant memories. At times, she had taken him in her arms and promised that someday they would have a lovely home of their own. She had made good that promise, for when he was in the third grade, they had moved here to Kelly's Landing.

Joseph had not understood then, but now that he was fourteen, he felt proud of his mother and respected her for her independence. He was beginning to feel some responsibility too. He worried sometimes about her working nights and coming home alone.

Joseph propped his bike near the hospital door and hurried inside. He could hardly wait to tell her what had happened. He found her on the second floor, reading charts at the nurses' station.

"Mother," he began as soon as he saw her, "you won't believe what just happened at school!"

"Baby," she exclaimed, "what's wrong? Are you okay?"

He hated it when she called him baby, but he let it pass.

"Yeah, I'm okay, but can we talk a minute?"

"Sure." She hurried toward him, then led him past the nurses' station and into a lounge area behind it. "What's wrong?"

Joseph let the whole story tumble out. She did not interrupt. When he had finished, she looked at him silently.

"Well," he asked, "what do you think? Do you think Huy and I are going to be in trouble?"

"Of course not," she assured him. "You didn't have anything to do with it, did you?"

"No, but we were the only ones there."

"That doesn't matter. I don't know what kind of mess this will turn into; but, if you didn't have anything to do with it, you don't have anything to worry about. I'm sure it will all be cleared up by tomorrow."

Joseph felt better. He had not admitted even to himself that he was a little scared.

"You think so?" he asked uncertainly.

"Sure. Don't worry about it, baby. It'll all work out."

"Mother . . ." Joseph's voice was stern.

"Okay, okay," his mother put in quickly. "I mustn't call you 'baby.' I know. I'm sorry. Okay?"

Joseph smiled at her. "Okay," he said.

She led him back toward the nurses' station. "We'll talk again tonight. Maybe I'll hear something about it here at the hospital. If so, I'll give you a call."

"I thought I would go down to Huy's right now. He is helping his father get the boat ready for Sunday. Maybe he can come to our apartment tonight. We'll wait up for you."

"You don't need to do that. I'll be all right."

"Sure. Just be careful."

She gave him a playful tap on the back. "Okay," she laughed, "and don't you turn into a worry-wart just because you are growing up."

Joseph turned and started for the elevator.

He retrieved his bike and rode to the beach, where he found Huy and his father just putting away their paintbrushes. Lonesome heard Joseph coming. He cleared the rail with one bound and landed on the dock. Joseph knelt down to hug him and was rewarded with a sloppy kiss and several licks on the face with a rough tongue.

"Good afternoon," Huy's father called from the deck. "It seems that our friend is very glad to see you."

11

"Good afternoon, Mr. Ta." Joseph stood up and bowed slightly toward the older man. Joseph had become familiar with the formal bows and greetings regularly observed by Huy's family.

Huy wiped the paintbrush that he was cleaning and wrapped it in a piece of newspaper. "Since we are finished here, Father, Joseph and I would like to exercise Lonesome along the beach for a while."

"Of course," Mr. Ta responded as he wrapped his own brush and put it away. "The lazy dog does nothing but sleep until you boys get home every day. He needs to be exercised or he will become fat and worthless." Although Mr. Ta spoke in a flat voice without looking at them, both boys knew that he really liked Lonesome and suspected that he gave the dog more affection and attention during the day than he would admit.

"Yes, sir," Huy said, winking at Joseph. "We shall go now, if that is all right."

"Yes, go. I will just finish putting these things away. We will have her ready for Sunday." Mr. Ta stepped back to admire the pilot house. "Just a few more touches to the trim and rails tomorrow, then your mother will help us with the decorations." He turned a bowed head toward the boys. "Yes, go, my son."

"Who do you think took that rock?" Joseph asked as they climbed across the big granite boulders which formed the long jetty. The rocky walkway extended out into Galveston Bay to prevent the shoreline from washing away.

"How would I know?" Huy answered. "It seems rather stupid to me. What could they do with it? They couldn't ever show it to anyone. Certainly, they couldn't sell it." He hesitated. "Unless they planned to take it out of the lucite pyramid. Do you think they could sell it then?"

"No way," Joseph said. "In the first place, who would believe it was a moon rock? It looked just like an earth rock to me."

"That's true," Huy agreed.

"Then, in the second place, don't you remember what the brochure from NASA said? Moon rocks don't get exposed to water or oxygen, so in our atmosphere they would do what the scientists call 'rust' very quickly. In the laboratory they are stored in dry nitrogen and the ones loaned out are encased in the lucite."

They had reached the point of the jetty. The two boys settled down on a large, flat boulder. Gulls circled overhead, tilting their white, black-tipped wings to the wind which tousled the boys' hair and billowed Huy's thin cotton shirt out in front of him. A late norther had blown in after Easter, bringing with it unusually chilling winds for April. Lonesome sniffed inquiringly along the cracks between the rocks and climbed down to the water's edge.

"I hate to tell my father about my jacket," Huy said sadly. "It will anger him."

"You haven't told him yet?"

"No."

"But it wasn't your fault," Joseph protested. "Surely he will understand that."

"Yes, he will understand, but he will be upset anyway. It has been hard since the bay waters were closed in December. But now, since the gulf waters are opening, perhaps things will be better. It is not pleasant for us Vietnamese at times. You would not understand."

"Yes, I do. I know that you get a hard time at school and the kids of the shrimpers act the worst sometimes. But they'll come around. They just don't know a good thing when they see it. I like you a whole lot, Huy."

Huy's dark eyes glowed as he smiled broadly. "Me too," he said. "Thank you, Joseph."

Joseph laughed. "And remember," he said, "just because I am an Anglo, that doesn't make me the most popular kid on the block. Short and stumpy with glasses don't a movie hero make." He shrugged again. "But about your jacket . . . you can have mine. I have another one almost like it at home."

13

"My father would not allow it."

"Tell him we swapped."

"My father doesn't allow lying either."

"Then, what?"

"We shall see when I get home."

Lonesome bounded up the jetty, face and front legs dripping with salt water. He shook, spraying both boys, then placed a wet paw on Joseph's shoulder.

"Okay, boy," Joseph said, getting up, "have you had enough?"

Lonesome jumped to the next boulder, stopped, and looked back.

"We're coming," Joseph assured him. "You know, Huy, about that moon rock . . . it had to be somebody that knows how to dispose of it. The job was too well-planned — waiting until just when the bell sounded and the halls got loud, bringing the duffel bag to tie up Miss Duncan — everything. Except your coat — that doesn't fit."

"Pun?" Huy laughed. "No, maybe that was planned too. Anyone who watched carefully could know that both of us take our things into Miss Duncan's office every day at the beginning of last period. We've done it all year."

"That's right," Joseph said thoughtfully. Suddenly, he started leaping across the boulders toward the shore. "Come on, let's go," he called.

Huy followed. He could see a couple, arm-in-arm, walking along the water's edge.

"Your sudden hurry wouldn't be because you see Jan coming, would it?" he laughed.

Jan Edwards was a senior, voted the most popular girl in the school, the tennis team's top player, and, Huy knew, the subject of many of Joseph's daydreams.

"Yeah. Is that that no-good Pete with her?" Joseph asked.

"It is, and he is a 'no-good,' for sure. Lately, he gives my father a bad time at the dock."

"Why doesn't your father report him to Mr. Kelly? He owns the docks."

"It wouldn't do any good. Mr. Kelly just takes Pete's side. I have heard that he has gotten him out of trouble with the police several times. He has just about taken him over as a son, I think, since Pete dropped out of school."

They neared the shore-end of the jetty and slowed down. Joseph waved. Jan smiled, waved and called something, but the wind took the sound away from them. Joseph lowered his arm.

"Mother said that Pete was brought to the emergency room on her last graveyard shift. He had been in a fight and was cut up some. He had a bunch of stitches. I sure didn't know that Jan went with him."

"Jealous?" Huy asked teasingly.

" 'Course not. She wouldn't have anything to do with me, anyway. You know that."

"But we can all dream, can't we?"

"Yeah, we can."

"I need to get home," Huy changed the subject. "I have to go to the store for my mother."

"I'll go with you and feed Lonesome. Mother's on the three-to-eleven shift at the hospital. Maybe you can come over to the apartment later and we can watch television."

"Okay, I'll ask my parents."

"Good. Maybe we can slip Lonesome in after dark."

When they reached the wharf where Huy's boat was moored, they found a general flurry of activity. Everyone was preparing for the Blessing of the Fleet, which would take place the following Sunday, and for the opening of the gulf shrimping season on Tuesday.

All the Vietnamese shrimpers docked their boats in the same area. Tall masts and upraised outriggers crisscrossed against the backdrop of sky and water. Green, blue, and white nets hung from these in graceful drapes, adding color to the irregular pattern. The strange, musical sounds of the Vietnamese language blended with the sounds of motors being tuned and gears being tested. The water between the U-shaped dock was crowded with

15

boats of various sizes. Their back, or aft, decks touched the dock and their sides touched one another. Old automobile tires tied to the black piles kept the boats from rubbing against the posts and damaging their hulls.

On the land side, shrimp houses, ice houses, diesel pumps, and net shops lined the wooden walkway. Joseph and Huy paused in front of one of the net shops to wave at LuAnn, one of their classmates. She was tying a green net at regular intervals to a cable which stretched the entire length of the narrow room. Her sister sat on the floor beside her, hammering flat wooden disks, called "flippers," along the bottom of the net. These flipped and rolled along the bottom of the water while round floats at the top held the net in a vertical position.

"Hi," LuAnn called, waving with the oval plastic net needle still in her hand. "Come on in. Dad will put you to work."

Joseph grinned and shook his head. "No thanks," he called back, "that is what we are afraid of."

The boys found Huy's mother and father both on board their boat at the far end of the dock. Mrs. Ta stood tying long strands of brightly colored string to a heavy net. The strings were called "whiskers" and the heavy net a "shaffing gear." It was designed to drag below the lighter fishing net and protect it from being snagged or torn by debris on the bottom.

Mrs. Ta looked up as they stepped on deck. She bowed her head toward them and spoke. "Isn't it beautiful?" she asked, lifting a portion for the boys to see. "I love the bright colors. So much prettier than the plain black and white that some use."

"Yes," Joseph agreed eagerly, "it looks sharp."

"It is a shame," she said thoughtfully, "that soon it will be all wet and muddy." She began skillfully tying on the whiskers again.

"But, when that happens, the nets will then be full of shrimp," said Mr. Ta reasonably, as he stepped out from the pilot house. "And I promise to wash them clean and bright again each time." He placed his hand affectionately on Mrs. Ta's arm.

"Father," Huy began, "if there is nothing that you need me to do now, would it be all right for me to visit Joseph this evening? We would like to study and watch television together."

Mr. Ta seemed to ponder the question thoughtfully.

"Yes," he answered. "Will you be late?"

"Joseph's mother gets home at eleven. She will bring me as she always does."

"That is good." He nodded his head. "It will be nice for you to keep Joseph company."

A remarkable contrast existed between the homes of the two boys. Joseph lived with his mother in one of the newest apartment complexes that had sprung up in Kelly's Landing in the past few years. It had a recreation room, gym, and swimming pool for the use of the tenants. The apartment was quiet, air-conditioned, and comfortable.

Huy lived in one of a group of summer cabins abandoned by their former owners after Hurricane Carla. Built up on high pilings, the cabins now stood cramped among a group of waterfront restaurants. Here, the most affluent citizens brought their land-locked friends to eat seafood and enjoy the view of the shrimp-boat docks and the sailboats that paraded past from the open bay to the fancy yacht club farther down the beach. Huy's cabin was too small for himself, his parents, and his three younger sisters. Crowded and noisy, its only air-conditioning was the constant sea breeze which brought with it dampness and salty residue.

Yet, to Joseph and Huy, this contrast meant nothing. They enjoyed their companionship in either place.

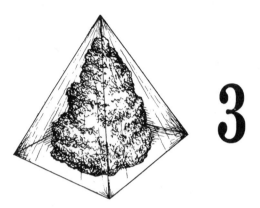

3

By the following morning, news of what had happened was all over town. There were two police cars parked in front of the school, and the local sheriff was pulled into the lot where the school buses unloaded. The sheriff stood near the door, directing the students to go inside to their first-period classroom and wait for further instruction.

Although Joseph walked to school, he arrived just as a bus was unloading and entered with the group. There was much excitement and talk. Questions called out to the sheriff went unanswered as students were hustled inside. There was nothing to do but speculate among themselves as to what was going on. Joseph listened and laughed to himself. Some of that speculation was definitely wild.

Later, Joseph settled down in his seat in the auditorium. The classes had marched in as groups at the beginning of first period. The unscheduled assembly had been announced over the public address system several minutes after school had begun. Joseph looked for Huy's class. They had assigned seats several rows ahead of his in the center section. It was easy to spot Huy's jet-black hair in the group.

"Students . . ." The P.A. system blared and then gave a high-pitched squeal. Mr. Greyson adjusted the microphone and blew into it.

"Whuff, whuff." Another squeal. "Students, let's all find our seats now and settle down. Settle down. We need to get started. Let's get started."

The talking and laughter quieted to a soft buzz as Mr. Greyson leaned toward the microphone again.

"Thank you. Thank you for taking your places so quickly. We have a very important matter to discuss with you this morning."

He lowered his voice and smiled at his audience.

"And I know that you are all eager to get back to your classes."

A concerted groan came from the students. After all, it was the expected response. Mr. Greyson always began his assemblies with this same attempt at humor.

Joseph turned his attention to the two men who sat behind Mr. Greyson on the stage. He immediately named one "Bushy Brows." Dark, thick eyebrows protruded above squinty eyes and a long, hooked nose. His face was ruddy and pockmarked. Gray, untidy hair touched his massive shoulders, reminding Joseph of one of the bull-like wrestlers that he had seen on Saturday-night TV. The man sat slumped toward the audience, his elbows resting on his knees.

If "Bushy Brows" were a bull, then the man seated beside him was more like a Labrador Retriever. Joseph suspected that he had once been an athlete. Sitting erect, of medium height and slender, his broad shoulders gave a hint of a muscular body beneath his suit. His early tan, sun-bleached hair, and dark brown eyes gave him the look of a man of the outdoors. Although he seemed to be relaxed, his eyes roved the audience and crinkled slightly at times as he smiled at individual students. His eyes rested on Joseph, and Joseph smiled back.

Mr. Greyson was introducing "Bushy Brows." He was Dr. Braun Wilhelm, chief scientist in charge of lunar specimens at the Johnson Space Center. The principal handed the microphone to Dr. Wilhelm, who spoke with a heavy accent.

"Good morning. As some of you may know, we have met today to discuss a crime that occurred in your school yesterday afternoon. A priceless national treasure has been stolen. I came here to impress upon you the gravity of such an act. The administration hopes that once the thief realizes the seriousness of his crime, the specimen will be returned and an investigation will not be necessary." He continued.

"I have with me Mr. Vincent Pierce, a federal investigator who will find the thief in case the specimen is not returned voluntarily. It may interest you to know that on one other occasion, this same incident happened and the rock sample came back by parcel post."

Joseph looked around at the audience and noted that not a single student was unattentive. They hung on every word of Dr. Wilhelm.

"The National Aeronautics and Space Administration has done everything possible to make those specimens available to the public," he continued. "Since Neil Armstrong and Buzz Aldrin first landed on the lunar surface in July 1969, twelve astronauts have explored the surface of the moon. They have collected rocks and soil samples from eight different places on the moon's surface. The laboratory now has more than two thousand separate samples amounting to eight hundred and forty-two pounds of lunar specimens.

"Many samples have been incapsulated in lucite, such as the one that you had displayed in your school, so that they may be seen and enjoyed by as many people as possible. Others are stored at the Johnson Space Center and are loaned out to scientists. At present, we have samples in sixty laboratories, fifteen of which are in foreign countries." Dr. Wilhelm paused and studied the audience intently.

"If anyone needs or wants a sample, he may go through channels to obtain one, but theft will not be tolerated. Do you have any questions?"

No one spoke. Dr. Wilhelm turned to take his seat.

"Dr. Wilhelm," a voice said from the audience. Joseph saw that it was Mr. Jones, the chemistry teacher. "You called the sample rock a priceless national treasure. Exactly what does that mean?"

Joseph had read all of the brochures that had come with the moon rock, and he had seen Mr. Jones reading them too. The term "priceless national treasure" had been fully explained. He knew that Mr. Jones was just breaking the ice, so that others would also feel free to start asking questions.

Dr. Wilhelm returned to the microphone and, for the first time, smiled.

"Well, actually, the name is a great misnomer. It really means that it costs more than one can calculate. For instance, to estimate the cost of the samples, one would have to include the entire Apollo program, which cost the taxpayers twenty-four billion dollars, the cost of the vaults built at the Johnson Space Center to house the samples, which was roughly one million dollars, and the yearly cost of the maintenance and staffing of that building, which right now runs about six-hundred thousand dollars per year. In other words, sir, we call a thing priceless when it costs so much that we don't want to think about it."

Since Dr. Wilhelm had smiled, the audience responded with a ripple of laughter.

"What would anyone do with the rock sample?" a student asked.

"That depends on the thief," he answered. "I suppose that there might be collectors who would be willing to hoard it and never let anyone know that they had such a prize. And, I suppose, there would be some people who

21

would do such a thing for thrill or notoriety. As I said, it would depend on the thief."

"Dr. Wilhelm . . ."

Joseph recognized the voice immediately. He turned and saw Jan standing with her hand raised.

"Yes?" Dr. Wilhelm said, pointing at her.

As she lowered her hand, she ran it nervously through her short blonde hair several times. It was a habit that Joseph knew well. He had watched her at tennis matches comb her hair with her fingers whenever the pressure was on.

"What will happen," Jan asked, "if the thief is caught?"

"That is not in my line. Let's let Mr. Pierce answer your question. He is our federal investigator."

Mr. Pierce took the microphone. "The person or persons responsible will be charged with grand theft and tried in a federal court."

"Would the person go to a federal prison?" asked a voice from the back row.

"If convicted," Mr. Pierce said, nodding his head.

"Do you have any suspects?" someone else asked.

"At this point, everyone is a suspect," he answered.

"Are students going to be called out of class to be questioned?" a teacher asked.

"From time to time this may occur, but not often. I will ask Mr. Greyson to provide a central area where I can work." He smiled and added, "We can conduct interviews before and after school and at lunch. So don't worry — I'll stay out of the way as much as possible."

Silence followed that statement. After a few moments, Mr. Greyson came to the microphone.

"Thank you, gentlemen. Dr. Wilhelm and Mr. Pierce have taken time away from their busy schedules to come and talk to you. We hope that they have impressed upon you the seriousness of this crime. If any of you are involved in this matter or have any information at all, any at all, here is your chance to go to Mr. Pierce and tell him what you know. We will return to our classes at this time."

When the groan which followed Mr. Greyson's statement died down, Jack Washington, the star forward on the basketball team, called out: "Reckon we're going to be on TV, Mr. Greyson?"

"I sincerely hope not," Mr. Greyson answered, rolling his eyes and lifting his hands. "Go back to your classes and we'll hope for the best."

A rumble of voices began as the students headed for the back of the auditorium. Joseph pushed up his seat and let the students on his row go out ahead of him. He wanted to wait for Huy. As the others passed, he could hear their remarks.

"According to my calculations, we have a twenty-four-billion, ten-million, two-hundred-thousand-dollar crime on our hands."

"Did you even look at it?"

"Yeah, but I didn't see that much to it."

"That Mr. Pierce is cute, isn't he? I wonder if he's married."

"Hey, Joseph, I heard that you were in the middle of it. Is that true?"

Joseph nodded to the last questioner and stepped out into the aisle as Huy approached.

"What do you think?" Joseph asked.

"I think that my jacket might have been used in a high crime."

"What did your father say about your losing it?"

"You would have thought that *it* was the priceless national treasure, the way he bemoaned its loss."

Joseph laughed.

As the boys neared the back of the auditorium, Joseph noticed Jan standing beside the door. She was looking directly at him and smiling.

"Your girlfriend is waiting for you," Huy said, nudging Joseph.

23

Joseph colored slightly. "You know she is not waiting for me."

"Well, if she's not, she surely is watching you right now."

Joseph was furious with himself because he could feel the blood rushing to his cheeks, but he managed to smile as he approached her.

"Hi, Jan."

"I have been waiting for you," Jan said, as she fell into step with them.

"Us? Really? Why?"

"Can't a girl wait to talk with her friends?"

"Friends . . . Gee, sure."

Huy put his hand on Joseph's shoulder. Joseph turned.

"It's okay, Joseph," Huy said, frowning slightly and backing away, "you two go on and talk. I'll see you at sixth period."

Jan dismissed Huy with a smile and a nod and then leaned closer to Joseph and ran her arm through his.

"I was sitting by Miss Duncan and I heard her tell one of the teachers that you and Huy and Jezebel were in the A-V room yesterday when this happened," she said.

"That's right," Joseph said, feeling very important, slightly embarrassed, and more than a little puzzled at this sudden attention. "Jezebel was giving Huy a rough time."

"Did y'all see anything?"

"No, we were in the equipment room."

"Didn't you even hear anything?"

"No, not until we heard Miss Duncan calling for help. By the time we got there, she was tied up in a duffel bag and all alone."

"I don't believe I know anyone named Jezebel. Is she new in school?"

"No," Joseph laughed. "She's not new; she's old, and she needs to be thrown away."

"Thrown away?"

"Yeah, she is an old foldup screen that everybody hates."

"Oh." Jan wrinkled her nose and looked at Joseph as though she was still not sure that she understood. "You mean Jezebel is a projection screen?"

"Right." Joseph nodded. "I guess it's kind of silly, but some of the teachers just started calling her that."

"Well, I was just wondering if you all had seen or heard anything unusual."

"No." Joseph stopped. The halls began to clear now, and he realized that he had passed his classroom door. "I've got to go to biology," he apologized, reluctant to have her remove her arm from his, "and we've already passed the lab."

"Oh, that's okay," Jan said. "I've got to get to English too. We'll talk again later."

"Gee, that'll be great!"

Joseph turned back toward the biology lab, squared his shoulders, stood taller, and practiced the nonchalant swagger that he had observed seniors using.

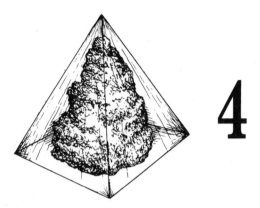

4

When Joseph entered the library at sixth period, he gave an audible groan. The tables in the reading room were strewn with books and magazines. Miss Duncan stood behind the charging desk, helping a line of students who wanted to check out books. Beside the charging machine lay a two-inch stack of unfiled book cards. The two student assistants from the last period were gathering up their own books and leaving.

"Sorry!" said one of them as she walked past Joseph. "We worked as hard as we could — honestly."

Some of the students standing in line before the charging desk must have decided that they did not have time to check out their books before the tardy bell rang. They turned to leave, dumping the books on various table tops on their way out.

Joseph groaned again.

"Wow!" said Huy, coming up behind him. "What a mess!"

"Yeah," Joseph agreed, "every teacher in school must have assigned term papers."

"Or," said Huy, nodding toward one of the glassed-in

conference rooms, "everyone just wants to know what's going on."

Inside the room, Mr. Pierce sat at the long table. He had changed his clothes since the morning assembly and now, dressed in blue jeans and a striped tee shirt, he looked relaxed and younger than he had appeared on the stage. Joseph could see him laughing with a student seated opposite him. The student unfolded his six-foot-two frame and stood up. It was Jack Washington. He leaned across the table and shook hands with Mr. Pierce. Then they walked together to the door.

"Don't forget to mention me to your friends," Jack said as he stepped into the reading room. "You never know when a good word might help."

Joseph couldn't hear Mr. Pierce's reply, but he saw him nod and make a "scout's honor" sign.

Without waiting for instructions from Miss Duncan, Joseph and Huy started to work. Huy shifted all of the books from one table to another. He began collecting the loose magazines and arranging them in alphabetical order on his clean work area. He would then be able to place them in order on the slanting display shelves.

Joseph went for a rolling, three-tiered book truck. He gathered the books from the nearest table and began placing them on the truck in Dewey decimal order. When the top shelf filled, he shifted half the books to the second shelf. A hand holding a book appeared on his left.

"Nine-twenty," a pleasant voice said. "Put it on the bottom shelf now and you won't have to shift it later."

Joseph looked up in surprise.

"Believe it or not," Mr. Pierce grinned, "I did this in college to help pay my expenses."

Joseph placed the book on the bottom shelf, shifted two other 900s next to it, and straightened up.

"Really?" he asked. "Maybe my friend Huy could do that. He really wants to go to college."

"Maybe so." Mr. Pierce handed Joseph another book. "Librarians are always looking for male students to do the heavy, dirty work. Where does Huy want to go to college?"

"Anywhere. He just wants to go."

"What sort of career is he interested in?"

"Well," Joseph frowned, then shrugged his shoulders, "we've talked about a lot of things. But mostly, I think, he just doesn't want to be a shrimper."

Mr. Pierce continued handing down the books from the table top, so Joseph sat on the floor in front of his truck and placed them in order.

"I understand you and Huy were working in the library yesterday when the theft occurred. Is that right?"

"Yes, sir, but we were in the audio-visual room. Did you want to talk to us about it now?"

A look of mock horror crossed Mr. Pierce's face as he pointed toward Miss Duncan. "And have that pretty lady after me for disturbing her workers? No, thanks! What will you be doing after school?"

"Huy and I mostly go down to the water. Sometimes we just fool around and play with my dog. And sometimes we have to help Huy's father on his boat."

"Would you mind if I came along with you this afternoon? We could talk then. Besides, I love beach areas and very rarely get a chance to just 'fool around' on one."

"Sure. That would be okay." The book truck was full and Joseph stood up. "I'll tell Huy and we'll wait for you."

"Good. Do you have another book truck?"

"In the A-V room. Why?"

"I'll shelve these. You go get another truck and fill it up."

Joseph watched Mr. Pierce move away, pushing the book truck before him. This was indeed a strange sort of federal investigator, not at all like the ones on TV. Joseph wondered if he liked to read and why he had chosen library work to help pay his way through college. Had he ever been short for his age as Joseph was now? He was not really tall, maybe five feet eight or nine. He was muscular, but not in a football or boxing sort of way. He looked more like a tennis player or a judo expert. Yeah. Joseph would be willing to bet that the man knew judo or karate or both.

Joseph resolved to put more time in practicing his own tennis game instead of hanging around the courts just to watch Jan play. Maybe his mother would let him take some karate lessons. He tried to picture himself looking as Mr. Pierce did, but thoughts of glasses, freckles, and unruly blonde hair somehow marred the image. He shrugged and started for another book truck.

Joseph passed the place where the moon rock had been displayed. The pictures of the astronauts were still in place with a neatly typed biography beside each one. There was a picture of all of the crew of the ill-fated *Challenger,* which had blown up shortly after takeoff. An account of the tragedy taken from the *Houston Post* lay on the table in front of it. Although these astronauts had nothing to do with the Apollo missions, Miss Duncan thought that they should be included in the display. Everything was there except the rock and the disk borrowed from NASA. Joseph wondered what Miss Duncan had done with the disk. When he passed Huy shelving magazines, he stopped.

"Mr. Pierce wants to go to our beach this afternoon," Joseph told him.

"For what reason, I wonder. Did he say?" Huy turned to look in Mr. Pierce's direction. "What is he doing? Shelving books?"

"Yeah, he's a nice guy. I'll tell you about it later."

Huy was not the only one surprised at the sight of the new library worker. Students who had come into the room for the last period to study, or "just to see what was going on," as Huy had suggested, were watching him. Even Miss Duncan raised questioning eyebrows.

By the time the dismissal bell sounded, the reading tables had been cleared except for the few books and magazines the students were still using. Huy had gone behind the charging desk and was dropping the last of the book cards into place.

While the halls echoed with the sounds of student voices and the metal clanging of lockers, the four left in the library worked silently and steadily until the last of the tables were cleared and the chairs were pushed neatly to the table edges. By the time they had finished, the halls were silent again. Miss Duncan smiled at them from behind the desk.

"Thank you so much," she said, looking around. "I must admit that I didn't think you could do it. I never saw such a day around here before. Mr. Pierce, I knew that Huy and Joseph were efficient, but you surprised me. We couldn't have done it without you."

"It was my pleasure," he assured her. "I haven't done this kind of work in a long time. I now admit to being one of the ones who mess up libraries instead of straighten them. And, by the way, my name is Vince. All of my friends call me Vince."

"Ann," said Miss Duncan simply.

"Ann, Joseph, and Huy." He looked at each of them in turn, then at his watch. "Twelve minutes. Would you say it took you about the same amount of time to finish up in the A-V room yesterday, boys?" he asked.

"Yes, sir, I guess so," Joseph hesitated, looking at Huy.

"Yes, sir," Huy agreed.

Mr. Pierce took a small notebook from his pocket, wrote in it for a moment, and then changed the subject abruptly.

"All of you must call me Vince," he said. "When someone says 'Mr. Pierce,' I always look around for my daddy." He made an exaggerated pantomime of looking behind himself. The others laughed.

"So, Ann," he continued, "may we walk you to your car? The boys have allowed me to invite myself to go to the shore with them. Maybe you would like to come with us?"

"No, thank you, to both questions," Miss Duncan shook her head. "My car is right outside and I need to get home. Can I give you all a lift?"

"How far is it?" Vince asked Joseph.

"Just a couple of blocks."

"Then we'll walk."

They all left the library together.

When the bell had sounded, Jan gathered her books together. She thought she would go by the library to see if Joseph had learned anything new about the theft. She had heard that the federal investigator had set up a temporary office in one of the library's conference rooms. Jan knew that Joseph had a crush on her, so she might as well use that to her advantage.

As she pushed the door open, Jan saw Joseph and Mr. Pierce shelving books. She blinked in surprise and frowned. Whatever was going on, this was not the time to question Joseph. She closed the door and headed for the parking lot, where she knew Pete Hebert would be waiting.

She found Pete in the usual place. When she reached for the door handle and opened the door, it swung easily for a few inches and stopped. Then, nothing but a hard jerk would budge it any farther. Jan gave it a mighty tug and cringed at the sharp metallic crack.

"Why don't you get this door fixed?" she said as she flopped into the front seat. "I am tired of wrestling with it. This car always did hate me."

"Forget the car and tell me what happened in the assembly today. It's all over town that a federal agent has been called in. Is that true?"

"Yes, he's here," she said, "and he means business." She ran her hand through her hair several times furiously. "This is a federal crime that you got me into and we can go to a federal prison for a long, long time — and not together, either!"

"Okay, okay, Jan. Lower your voice and take it easy." He started the engine and eased into the after-school traffic. "Let's ride around and talk."

"Why didn't you tell me how serious this rock business would be? I would have never helped you."

"You seemed anxious enough when you thought your cut would furnish your dream trip to Wimbledon in June. Anyway, we're not going to get caught. Mr. Kelly will take care of us, don't worry."

"You hope! When that German-sounding man introduced the investigator in the assembly, he made it clear that the thief would be caught, unless the rock was brought back voluntarily. He acted just like there was no question about it. Pete, we've got to take it back."

"You're wrong, baby. We can't take it back. We are already in too deep."

"But the man said if it were returned voluntarily, there would be no investigation. He even told us how to do it. He said that one had been returned by mail. They act like they don't really want to know who did it so much; they just want the rock back."

"That may be true, but we might be safer in a federal prison right now than we will be if I don't turn that rock over to Mr. Kelly."

"What can he do?"

"Anything he wants to, baby. If we just stay cool and turn the rock over to his buyer next Sunday, he can protect us. But if we panic now, he can take care of us in another way. Believe me! He has more than shrimpers and dock hands working for him. That much, I do know. Do you remember that kid from Houston that was supposed to have overdosed and run off the bridge about six months ago?"

"Yes, but what does that have to do with anything?"

"Well, it just so happens that the same kid was messing around in his motor boat the night the Vietnamese shrimp boat was burned out in the harbor. He saw what happened, but he never made it home to tell about it."

"Do you mean Mr. Kelly . . .?"

"Yes, I mean Mr. Kelly. Not him, but his hired goons."

"How do you know that?"

"I just know — believe me. And the less you know, the better."

Jan ducked her head and brushed away tears. Her voice broke.

"Oh, Pete, I'm really scared."

"Don't worry, baby. Just play it cool. I'll take care of you."

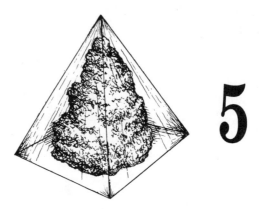

5

The beaches at Kelly's Landing were unlike those farther down Galveston Bay and along the Gulf of Mexico. Joseph and Huy always referred to it as "the beach," mainly because they liked the idea of having a beach to walk on. Most of the people in town, however, referred to it as "the water's edge," which, in fact, was a more accurate name.

The town was built on a low bluff which stood some twelve to fifteen feet above sea level and protected the residents from any normally high tide. In most places between the bluff and the water, a narrow strip of grassy flat land divided the two. But in other spots, little more than fifteen or twenty feet of muddy bottom emerged from the sea at low tide. At high tide the waves licked and ate away at the land, causing cave-ins along those banks which were unprotected by manmade bulkheads or jetties. Boat landings and docks were built by having truckloads of oyster shell dumped along the muddy ground. With use, this shell was gradually broken and crushed into a very satisfactory pavement-like surface. It was also used for many of the roads and driveways in the area.

Joseph tried to explain all of this to Mr. Pierce as they walked past the wreckage from the last hurricane. Then, gesturing in a wide arc with his arms, Joseph explained the scene before them. With lively body language and voice sound effects at times, he rendered a colorful description of the hurricane, Alicia, that had rampaged along their coast. Vince listened intently as Joseph gave detail after detail of the remaining wreckage which included a restaurant, Meeks pier and bait store, and several beach houses.

He told about the rain falling, not downward but horizontally, and the roaring, violent wind and water as it threatened and claimed building after building, mobile homes, and boats of all sizes.

"And the birds," he said in wonder, "they disappeared the day before the storm came in. It was weird and very quiet without them."

"Those sea gulls on those old foundation pilings look like guards perched there now to sound the next warning," Vince mused thoughtfully. "The sea can be a mighty foe, can't it?"

"Yeah," Joseph answered, "but it's pretty good most times."

"It is for us, nearly all of the time," Huy added.

"I have two loyal sea-loving friends, I think," Vince concluded.

Both boys smiled.

"I guess this is not the kind of beach you are used to, huh?" Joseph asked.

"To tell you the truth," Mr. Pierce replied, "I am not used to any sort of beach at all."

"Do you live in Washington?"

"Most of the time. I travel a lot."

There was a short silence. Joseph kicked a plastic cup as he, Huy, and Vince Pierce strolled along. Lonesome bounded after it but, after a few sniffs, decided it was not worth retrieving. He capered ahead or circled the walkers by turns. Often he waited, panting, while the others caught up.

"Gee, I never thought that you would like to go walking with us," Joseph said shyly. Huy nodded in agreement.

"Sure, I love to walk. And if there is water to walk beside, it is even better. Do you come here every day?"

"Every day that there is not a tennis practice," Huy stated, grinning.

Mr. Pierce lifted his eyebrows questioningly.

"Do you like tennis?"

"Yeah, it's okay," Joseph shrugged. "Mostly, I just like to watch."

Huy grinned broadly this time. "It's according to who is playing."

"Oh, and who do you go to watch, Joseph?"

Huy answered for him. "Jan Edwards. She is our senior tennis star and may even be up for a sports scholarship this year."

"Mr. Pierce," Joseph asked, "Huy didn't have to tell you that, did he? We don't have to answer every single question, do we?"

"No, you don't. By the way, I thought we decided that you would call me Vince."

"Yeah, thanks, Mr. Pierce . . . I mean, Vince," Joseph beamed.

"Mr. Pierce, I will not be permitted to call you Vince in front of my parents. It is not allowed," said Huy. "What is your middle name? My family will want to know."

"Are you ready for this?" Vince asked. "Vincent Isaac Pierce. Isn't that impressive?"

"Yeah, it is." Joseph was delighted. "You're a VIP — a very important person."

"Not really, but my mother thinks so. She still calls me Vincent Isaac."

Huy grinned. "So, I am not the only one who lives

with formalities in the home. I will call you Vince when we are on the beach, but Mr. Pierce at other times, okay?"

"Okay, that's a deal."

"Me too," Joseph said.

The three had reached the dilapidated Meeks fishing pier. Before the big storm, three years ago, it had been a popular place. About halfway out were the remains of the small room which had been used as a store. Here, Mr. Meeks had sold fishing tackle, bait, cold drinks, and straw hats to the tourists who had come unprepared but who wanted to try their hands at catching the big speckled trout. Mostly, they just caught drum and hardheads. The store and part of the pier still stood out in the water, but the piles and the platform which had once connected it to the land were gone. The winds and tides had taken away much of it in the storm. Since then, campers had used what was left to fuel their campfires. When the tide was out, as it was now, one could wade almost to the old store.

Lonesome sniffed and barked at the water's edge, his nose pointing out to sea.

"What's he barking at?" Vince asked.

"I don't know," Joseph answered. "Here, Lonesome, come."

Lonesome ignored the call, barked once, then splashed into the water. He swam straight to one of the piles beneath the old store and circled it several times, whining and yipping as he paddled about.

"I hope there isn't a jellyfish or a stingray out there," Joseph said, running toward the water's edge.

"Come, Lonesome, come!"

Lonesome circled the pier once more and started reluctantly toward Joseph. When he reached the shore, he shook the water from his long, shiny coat. Joseph stepped back until the spray was settled and then met Lonesome halfway and patted him on the head.

"Come on, boy, there's not anything out there that

37

you need." Huy and Vince smiled as they walked up to meet Joseph and Lonesome.

"Now," Vince said, "let's get back to this Jan Edwards. Wasn't she the one in the assembly this morning who asked what would happen to the thief? She is very pretty. You have good taste, my friend."

Joseph blushed. "You knew that? How did you know that? Did you memorize all of the questions?" he asked incredulously.

"No, I wrote them down as they were asked. Then your principal gave the names to me."

"Oh," Joseph said, "you started your investigation before you were ever introduced, didn't you? What else do you know?"

Vince laughed. "I don't have to answer every single question, do I?"

The boys laughed too.

"But I will tell you that a good investigator begins his investigation the minute that the assignment is made. I did a lot of reading last night about the history and the geography of this area."

"Do you know about my people?" Huy asked shyly.

"Yes, I know some things. I know that your people have had a hard time both in your own country and here."

"Do you blame us for wanting to come here, as many do?"

"No, but I can understand what makes some people feel the way they do about it."

"What? I wish I could understand."

"The Vietnam War was a very unpopular war in this country. In the first place, most Americans felt that it was none of our business and that we had no right to interfere with your country's internal affairs."

"But you have helped others who were oppressed by the Communists," Huy argued logically.

"Yes, but those wars were not popular either. It was not like the two world wars, when we went into it with

38

the intent of winning the war ourselves. Actually, we went to South Vietnam only to advise your people. But our boys ended up fighting, being killed, and taken as prisoners. We are still learning how much damage the veterans suffered from chemicals such as Agent Orange. It is natural that some people would still feel resentment. Can you understand that?"

Huy nodded his head slowly. "Yes. I guess I can understand that. But is that any reason for them to burn our boats, or try to make it impossible to make a living from these waters?"

"There is no reasoning whatsoever in retaliation. It is just the way some folks handle their emotions. It solves nothing and just causes more pain. How old were you when your family left South Vietnam?"

"I was three years old, but I remember it. We were boat people. The Americans saved us. They took us aboard their ship and fed us and gave medical help to those who needed it."

"Yeah, Huy's been relocated twice," interrupted Joseph. "He used to live in Port Isabel, but there were so many problems with the townspeople that the government moved them here."

"Yes, there have been problems everywhere. With ten million refugees, I suppose that was to be expected. Things are a bit better now, and time will take care of more," Vince said.

As they approached Mr. Ta's boat, he hailed to them from the deck. Lonesome raced ahead, leaped onto the deck, and headed for his favorite spot — a heavy coiled rope. It was his special place to curl up and sleep.

"Come aboard," Mr. Ta invited. "I see you have brought a friend."

Huy introduced Vince to his father. Mr. Ta bowed, smiling and extending his hand in greeting.

"It is a great pleasure to meet you," he said.

"Thank you," Vince answered, stepping onto the deck of the shrimp boat. "I am glad to meet you also. I have been visiting with your son and Joseph. They have been telling me of some of the problems with the other shrimpers."

"Yes, but we make it all right. What business are you in, Mr. Pierce?"

"I'm an investigator. I'm here to investigate the moon rock theft. I suppose you have heard what happened."

"I did indeed, from my son. I hope that you will remember, also, that my son's coat was stolen at the same time. Perhaps you will be able to find and return it."

"Yes, Mr. Ta, I shall certainly try."

Joseph suppressed a grin at the conversation about the coat. Huy had said that his father considered it more important than the moon rock.

"This is a fine boat you have here, Mr. Ta." Vince looked up and about. The freshly painted pilot house above him contrasted sharply with the weathered sides of the restaurants and fish houses which lined the shore behind it. Black trim around the high small windows which circled the pilot house still shined in spots where the new enamel had not yet dried. Scrubbed and sanded, the rails encircling the back deck awaited the paint which Mr. Ta had said he intended to apply the following morning.

"Thank you." Mr. Ta looked around in satisfaction. "She does look nice now, doesn't she? Of course, she will not be so neat and clean when we begin shrimping after next Sunday. Will you be here to see the Blessing of the Fleet, Mr. Pierce?"

"Perhaps. I hope so. I have never seen it before."

"Oh," Mr. Ta clasped his hands and nodded his head to emphasize his words. "Then you must plan to stay. It is beautiful. My wife has been making silk and paper flowers for weeks. She will have the nets, mast, and rails almost completely covered with them." He looked up to where the heavy nets draped gracefully from the upraised outriggers.

"Everyone will make his boat as beautiful as possi-

40

ble. Some even string colored lights about the pilot house and rails. It is lovely to see the boats lined up and passing before the priest to receive his blessing. It is also comforting to know that prayers are being raised to God for a good harvest and the safety of the men who work the boats."

"Are you a Catholic, Mr. Ta?"

"Oh, yes. My father before me worked with the missionaries in the old country." Mr. Ta paused thoughtfully for a moment, then finished quickly. "Yes, he chose to stay behind and finish his work when the rest of us left."

Vince, his eyes reflecting sympathy and understanding, started to speak but evidently changed his mind. He walked over to where a net lay draped across doors which opened into a hold. During shrimping runs, ice and freshly caught shrimp were stored in the hold. He ran his hand across the rough webbing.

"That's the try net," Joseph offered quickly, proud of the knowledge he had picked up on the few times he had been out shrimping with Huy and his father.

"Yes," Mr. Ta confirmed. "Ordinarily it hangs from the rigging, but Mrs. Ta wants it here in order to tie more flowers." He smiled as if to assure Mr. Pierce that it was out of place only to indulge his wife. "You know, perhaps, how wives are?"

"No, I don't," Mr. Pierce laughed, "but I can imagine." He turned toward Joseph. "Why is it called a try net?"

"Because it is the net to try first to see if there is enough shrimp caught to pull in the main nets."

"Very logical."

"Let me show you how it works." Joseph came over and began to explain enthusiastically. "See, you gather up the bottom and tie it with a sack knot right here. Then you let it drag the bottom just like the main nets. When you want to see how many shrimp you are catching, you haul it up, let it hang right up there," he pointed. "Then, you stand way back over here," he walked up toward the pilot house, "pull the knot, and the net dumps the catch on the deck."

"Very good, Joseph," Mr. Ta said. "Perhaps I shall hire you as my rigger someday."

Joseph wrinkled his nose and made a face toward Mr. Pierce. "Well," he said, shrugging his shoulders, "it is really not all that much fun. The net brings more than just shrimp in — mud and slime, fish, crabs, stingrays. It is really a pretty big mess."

"Yes, Joseph, you are correct again," Mr. Ta said. "I am afraid, Mr. Pierce, that neither of these boys have any ambitions to become a shrimper." He looked from one to the other. "Nor can I blame them," he said sadly. "It is a hard life with few rewards. It is a universal hope of parents, I believe, that their children will have a better life than they have had. But, enough of this talk." He turned to Vince. "Let me show you the pilot house."

Joseph and Huy followed and listened proudly as Mr. Ta guided Vince around. The pilot house was Joseph's favorite part of the shrimper. It was the shape of an elongated oval, cut in half, with the door and one window on the straight, back side. The other sides and the curved front had small windows encircling the interior with very little space between. Every inch of the cabin had a designated use. Aside from the ship's wheel and instrument panel, there were various ship-to-shore radios, each with different wavelengths. A counter top and cabinet held a hot-plate, nonperishable foodstuffs, and a locker with manuals and maps. A tall stool and foldup chair completed the furnishings.

Tucked discreetly between two window facings, along with the official permits and licenses, hung a small handcrafted plaque, its message carved in Vietnamese characters. Vince voiced his admiration of the artwork as he ran his fingers over the letters.

"What does it say?" he asked.

"It is a Psalm of David," Mr. Ta answered. "It says, 'Thou dost make him to rule over the works of Thy hands: the birds of the heavens, and the fish of the sea, whatever passes through the paths of the sea.' To me," he added, "it is a bit like a deed or a permit from God." He laughed. "The permits from the government are a little harder to obtain."

Vince smiled at this and nodded in agreement.

Joseph and Huy stayed with the two men in the small space until Lonesome wedged his body inside and switched and bumped first one and then the other with his wagging tail. It definitely became too crowded, and they all emerged onto the deck. Mr. Ta turned to Mr. Pierce.

"Perhaps you would like to go up to the house for tea. My wife would be honored to meet you."

"That would be very nice," Vince replied. "I would be honored to meet her too."

Mr. Ta stood back until the others had stepped onto the dock, then led the way toward the house. The steep stairs leading up to the living quarters smelled of fresh paint. Laundry hung across the rails of the porch and from thin ropes which stretched between the pilings that supported the house. Mr. Ta carefully wiped the soil from his shoes on a mat at the bottom of the steps. The others repeated his example.

"Mrs. Ta," Mr. Ta called from the top of the stairs. "We have a guest."

He opened the door and stood back for the others to enter. Mrs. Ta stood arranging silk flowers at a table in the center of the room. She was attaching them carefully around an opening in a metal box. Inside, she had placed a cross, a small candle, and a prayer book. Dropping the flowers on the table, she bowed toward the men.

Neither the bow, nor the greeting, nor the beautiful silk flowers were seen by Joseph, Huy, or Vince. Their eyes were riveted on the metal container. Plainly on the side were the letters: NASA.

"That's it!" Huy whispered. "That's the container for the moon rock!"

6

After a moment of complete silence, Mrs. Ta, who had turned expectantly to greet her guests, saw Huy, Joseph, and the men staring at her newly made creche.

"Do you like?" she asked in a quiet, questioning voice.

"My mother, where . . . how . . . did you get that?" Huy stammered.

Mrs. Ta smiled. "I made it, my son. Don't you recognize the cross and the prayer book?"

Joseph looked quickly at Vince. Vince's eyes swept the room, pausing to rest on Mrs. Ta several times. He started toward the container.

"Huy does not mean the articles in your creche, Mrs. Ta," he said, placing his hand on the container, "he means this — where did you get this?"

"Why, from Mr. Ta," she answered, turning toward her husband.

The puzzled expression on Mr. Ta's face faded into one of disbelief.

"Do you mean that this box contained the moon rock that was stolen?"

"Yes, Mr. Ta. That is what we mean." Vince took out a note pad and compared his notes with the inventory code on the box. "How did this come into your possession, Mr. Ta?"

Joseph swallowed hard. His mouth had become dry with fear. There stood the container. It had probably left the library wrapped in Huy's coat. He and Huy had been the only ones in the library when the rock was stolen. Were he and Huy now suspects? He tried to read Huy's face. Huy, he knew, strived so diligently to fit into the American way of life; and yet he worried constantly about possible disgrace to his family. What was he thinking now?

Even under the circumstances, Mr. Ta continued with the introduction of his wife.

"Mr. Pierce, this is my wife, Mrs. Ta."

"Yes, I know, but let's get back to the subject of this box." Vince tapped it with his note pad.

Mrs. Ta backed away and drooped her head.

"Mr. Pierce," Mr. Ta's voice sounded strained, "I have twice tried to introduce you to my very good wife, and twice you have been more attentive to this box. I found the box this morning and gave it to my wife. Do you think if I had stolen it, I would have invited you into my home to view it?"

Joseph noticed that Huy and Mrs. Ta bowed slightly toward Mr. Ta. It was as if they were thanking him for reminding Vince of his lack of courtesy. Joseph felt a bit like applauding too. He had never heard Mr. Ta speak so forcefully before. Perhaps this Vincent Isaac Pierce wasn't the nice guy that he appeared to be. However, he began to apologize immediately.

"Yes, you're right," he said. He walked over and took Mrs. Ta's hand in his. "I am sorry, Mrs. Ta. It is a beautiful creche. It was just the shock of seeing the rock container that caused my rudeness. Forgive me."

"Of course," she smiled.

Vince turned back to the box.

"You realize, of course, that I will have to take this with me," he said, removing the cross, prayer book, and candle from inside. "It is evidence. I suppose that you cleaned it thoroughly — am I right?"

"Oh, yes," she beamed. "I washed away all of the dust, inside and out."

"That figures." He shook his head. "Mr. Ta, where did you find it?"

"Underneath the house. It was there this morning when I went down. We live so near the restaurants that I must clean up each day. People have so little respect. I pick up beer bottles, papers, and other unwanted trash all the time."

"Did you hear anything unusual last night?"

"No. We have learned to tune out the outside noises."

"There's no use to check for fingerprints, is there?" asked Joseph.

"Probably not, but we'll go ahead and check anyway. As a matter of fact, I should go. Thank you, Mr. Ta. At least you have found one piece of evidence."

With that, Mr. Pierce picked up the box, said his goodbyes, and left.

As soon as Mr. Pierce was out of sight, Joseph, Huy, and Lonesome left too. There were so many questions to ask each other, but so few answers. Why did the evidence keep revolving around Huy and his family? Was someone deliberately trying to involve them in the crime? The boys discussed the series of events over and over, but neither could come up with an answer.

Lonesome's barking broke into their discussion. They realized that they were back at Meeks pier, and Lonesome was reacting exactly the same way as before. He was standing at the water's edge, barking toward the old store.

"What do you suppose is out there?" Huy asked.

"I don't know," Joseph said, "but whatever it is, it is

still there. If it had been something in the water, it would have been gone by now. I'm going to go see."

Huy hesitated. "The water's going to be cold, and the tide is coming in."

"Nah," Joseph said, "it won't be bad. The heater for the school pool has been broken for weeks. I've been going in it every day. Besides, everybody went in on 'Splash Day' at Galveston during spring break." He began taking off his shoes and socks. "Whatever it is, I'm going to go check it out."

Huy began to take his clothes off too. "Okay. I'm game if you are."

Clad only in tee shirts and briefs, they waded out toward the pier. Mud oozed between their toes, and occasionally they felt a crab or fish brush their legs. The tide was rising and waves slapped their chests in regular rhythm. They could feel a slight seaward pull at their feet each time a wave passed. As the water deepened, it took only a small jump just before a wave hit to float their bodies over the swell, then set their feet back down on the muddy bottom. By the time they reached the pier, the water between waves reached their chests. Lonesome swam along beside them. The dog rounded the pier first and snapped at an object just above his reach.

The boys followed and soon saw what Lonesome was after. There, caught on a rusty nail, hung a scrap of material.

"That came off of my jacket!" Huy said.

"Are you sure?" asked Joseph.

Huy reached and took the scrap from the nail and held it toward Lonesome.

"Sure I am. Lonesome is too, aren't you, boy? See, here is my mother's stitching where she mended it last week." He gave the scrap to Lonesome and Lonesome headed toward the shore with it in his mouth.

"But, how did it get here? You don't suppose . . ." Joseph looked up, stretching his arm toward the old walkway. It was well beyond his reach. The black pilings would be impossible to climb, for they were heavily encrusted with sharp barnacles. He waded underneath the pier. There, near the place where the old store opened onto the pier, was a trap door and a rude ladder leading to it. Neither boy spoke. They both started up the ladder.

Joseph pushed back the trap door and crawled into the gloom of the old store. The sun had set and in the early twilight, the interior of the store was filled with dampness and shadows.

Joseph looked around and saw Huy's head appear through the trap door. "Come on," he urged. "This is scary."

"Then why are we here? And why are you whispering?" asked Huy.

"Yeah, why am I whispering?" Joseph answered, relaxing a bit and looking around.

At first the room appeared to be empty, but on closer examination, they found that someone had been there recently. Two cigarette butts were ground out on the floor, and a discarded candy wrapper was wadded up in the corner.

The boys walked behind the dilapidated counter — and there on the floor lay Huy's coat and a duffel bag like the one used to tie up Miss Duncan! Both boys knew what the bulge in the bag was. Huy went to work on the knot and soon had the lucite-encased rock in his hands.

"Wow! How do you suppose it got here?" Huy exclaimed.

"I don't know," Joseph said, "but we'd better get it back to Mr. Pierce."

"Yes," Huy agreed. "Maybe, we can — " Huy stopped and looked at Joseph. The expression on his face changed from mere astonishment to true anxiety. "Joseph, we can't," he said emphatically. "What if someone saw us with it?"

Joseph could not understand Huy's fear.

"What if they did? We'll tell them where we found it. We'll be heroes."

"No," Huy said sharply, "you don't understand. Can't you see that if I am caught with the rock now, everyone will believe that I stole it? Just think about it. We were in the library when the rock was stolen. The rock was taken out of the library in my jacket. The container was found at my house. If I am caught with it now, there is no way that anyone would believe that I didn't take it and that you didn't help me."

Joseph let the truth of Huy's words sink in. He felt a sudden chill that was deeper than the sea breeze against his wet skin. Huy was right. Not even Mr. Pierce would believe them. He seemed friendly enough, but Joseph remembered how his manner had changed when he discovered the container at the Ta home.

"Yeah, that's right. What do you think we should do?"

Huy shivered. The room darkened abruptly as if a cloud had covered the last rays of the setting sun. The sea breeze whistled through the cracks of the old store. The boys, in silence, pondered the weight of the problem.

"Let's just leave it. It's getting dark and we are both cold. Your teeth are even chattering. We'll go tell Mr. Pierce what we found," Huy suggested.

"What if whoever put it here comes back to get it while we're gone?"

"It would be better than being caught with it ourselves. I'll put it back in the duffel bag and leave it just like we found it. Now, let's get out of here."

Lonesome was waiting for them on the shore when they waded in, the scrap of the jacket still in his mouth. Joseph took it from him.

"I guess you're the real detective," he said, patting him on the head. "You're the one that really found the moon rock."

At the edge of the bluff, the boys hustled into their dry clothes. Suddenly, they heard the sound of a car pull up and park on the bluff above them. There was silence for a moment and then a sharp metallic crack. Huy looked at Joseph.

"That sound . . ." he whispered, "that's the same sound we heard the day of the robbery."

Joseph nodded. He finished tying his shoe and walked out from under the shelter of the bluff and looked up. Jan was just stepping out of Pete's car. Pete still sat at the wheel.

Jan! Could it have been Jan and Pete who had stolen the rock? Nah, it was just a coincidence. After all, lots of car doors were slamming outside the library that afternoon. But what were they doing here? Was this a coincidence too?

When Pete saw Joseph, he piled out of the car and started down the steep path, sliding occasionally on the wet earth. He looked around suspiciously when he got to the bottom.

"What do you boys think you are doing here?" he asked roughly.

"Nothing," Joseph said.

"Do you do nothing down here this time of night often?"

"Sometimes," Joseph answered.

Pete looked over at Huy, who still stood in the shelter of the bluff.

"You're not very particular about the company you keep, I see."

Joseph felt his anger rising. "Huy is my friend," he said defiantly.

"Well, take your friend and get outta here!"

An angry retort came to Joseph's mind, but he did not speak. He looked up at Jan.

"Oh, Pete," Jan called down, "let the boys alone. They're not hurting anything."

"I'll hurt them, if they don't get outta here."

This was too much for Joseph.

"It's a public beach. I guess we can come here when we want to."

Pete walked over and towered above him. Lonesome took offense at this and ran over to Joseph's side. He gave a menacing growl and Pete stepped back a bit but continued sarcastically.

"Not if I say you can't," he said. "I'd sure hate for anything to happen to the boat of your friend here. You know there's been lots of trouble on these Vietnamese boats lately, a fire here, a slashed net there. You know how it is."

At this, Huy took his place beside Joseph and Lonesome. Though he said nothing, his mouth was set in defiance and his eyes never wavered from Pete's face.

"Upset you a little bit, huh?" Pete taunted. "You rather we talk about Joseph a little? I understand his mother works at the hospital. Right? I believe that she was on the 'graveyard' shift a couple of weeks ago when I was in there. It'd be too bad if something happened to her on the parking lot some night."

"Pete, for heaven's sake!" It was Jan breaking in from the top of the bluff. "The boys haven't done anything. Let them alone."

"Okay," Pete growled. "I'm done with them just as soon as they leave."

Joseph wanted to lash back angrily, but he knew it would do no good. From his friendship with Huy, he had learned acceptance. Angry words never solved a problem.

"Come on . . . let's go," he said.

When the boys were out of earshot of Pete, Joseph grabbed Huy's arm.

"What do you think? Do you think he knows we were out there?"

"I don't know about that. He probably suspects, all right."

"He . . . and Jan . . . stole it, didn't they?" Joseph could hardly make himself include Jan in the question.

"I'm afraid so. At least, it sure looks that way. I am sorry, Joseph — about Jan, I mean."

"Me too." Joseph was silent for a few moments.

"Come on, let's go to my house. Mother can take you home when she comes in."

"Okay, but let's go by and ask my parents."

After they got to Joseph's apartment, they did not turn on the television, as was their habit. They discussed over and over the events of the last two days. In spite of the circumstantial evidence, and the threats made by Pete, they were in full agreement to tell the whole thing to Mr. Pierce the following morning.

The decision, however, was abruptly changed when Joseph's mother came home.

"Joseph," she said, as she entered, "I have had such a scare. My car was broken into and the doors were left wide open. I found it like that when I started home!"

Joseph gasped. "Mother, are you all right?"

"Yes, but who would do such a thing?"

Joseph looked at Huy and shook his head. They both knew that the secret they shared would have to be kept a secret. There was no way that they could tell Mr. Pierce now.

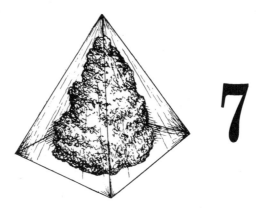

7

Watching the boys until they were out of sight, Jan felt a quiver of fear. This was a side of Pete that she had never seen. Finally, she spoke.

"Weren't you a little rough on them?"

"No. Not rough enough, probably."

"Oh, Pete, any rougher and you would have done them bodily harm."

"I'll do that, too, if I have to," he mumbled. He poked around the grassy area under the bluff. "Jan, throw down my flashlight," he called. "No, never mind, I'll come up and get it."

Jan wondered at his change of mind. Usually he was quick enough to send her on errands or have her wait on him. Maybe he was afraid he couldn't catch it in the darkness, although it was still light enough for him to see that well. She waited as he plodded up the rutted path.

"I could have gotten it," she said, following him to the car.

"I'll get it myself." Pete made an impatient gesture. "You go on back."

"Back? Back where?"

"Back on the bluff, back anywhere. Go watch for the boys."

Jan did not argue, but neither did she understand Pete's mood.

He soon returned, with flashlight in hand.

"I'm going back down to look around. Do you want to come with me?"

"No, I don't want to get dirty. I'll stay here. Are you going to be there long?" she asked, shivering. "It's cold."

"No, I won't be long."

Pete descended the slope once again. Jan could see him pointing the light around the area where he and the boys had their confrontation. Suddenly, she saw the excited bobbing of the light as Pete grabbed an object off the muddy embankment. She heard Pete swear vehemently. What was wrong?

"Jan, I've got to go out to the old store. I'll be right back. Get in the car and lock it."

"Pete, please don't go out there. It's too dark."

Pete did not wait for her reply. He slipped off his shoes and began wading toward the pier.

Jan got in the car on the driver's side. She was more than a little irked at Pete at this moment. She looked in her purse for an emery board and filed her nails. She wanted to play the radio, but Pete had the keys. Maybe he had some gum in the glove compartment. She tried to open it, but it was locked. In aggravation, she hit it with her fist and it popped open.

Since the door opened of its own accord, she reasoned, she might as well look inside. It did not take much looking to find out why Pete did not want her to look for the flashlight. There, under a raft of paper, lay a pistol! Why a pistol? She closed the compartment and began a high-level worry session. She was lost in thought when Pete finally returned.

"I'm sorry, baby, I just had to check on the moon rock. It was there, all right, but I think your little boy-

55

friends may know it's there. I found a scrap from that jacket down under the bluff."

"Oh, no! Are you going to do anything to them?"

"Not yet, but we do need to go see Mr. Kelly."

"Are we going to his house?"

"Sure. He told me to contact him anytime I needed to."

Jan and Pete rode in preoccupied silence to the Kelly mansion. Situated on a point on the south end of town, it stood out like an obese beacon to boats approaching it from the bay. It was said that old man Kelly had selected the site, surrounded as it was on three sides by water, in order to protect his rum-running business. It had been first built by the present Mr. Kelly's great-grandfather. Each succeeding generation had built onto it to suit their particular needs and tastes. Now it stood as a massive spread of wings and outbuildings and an architectural monstrosity.

Nestled among azaleas and yucca, the house stood three stories high. On each level, facing the bay, was a widow's walk, so named because women once used them to scan the horizon for a sail that would announce the return of their husbands. Now these screened porches were used for recreation and lounging. The side facing the road followed a pattern after the ante-bellum homes of the old South. White columns graced the wide veranda.

Pete turned in the curving drive between the oleanders that obscured the entrance from the road.

As he stopped in front of the veranda, two Dobermans trotted to the edge of the porch, alert and threatening.

"I'm not getting out of this car, Pete." Jan had no real fondness for dogs, and she had no desire to make friends with these monsters.

"Oh, these dogs won't hurt you. They know me." Pete got out of the car and came around to her side. He spoke to the dogs. They stood at attention but made no aggressive moves.

56

Reluctantly, Jan slid out of the car and grabbed Pete's arm. She followed him to the steps, then sidled around in front, always careful to keep him between her and the watchful pair. Pete punched the doorbell.

A Mexican-American servant took them to Mr. Kelly, who was in the den watching a basketball game on a large-screen television. Mr. Kelly lay sprawled in a lounge chair. The warm-up suit he wore did nothing to hide the rolls of fat which circled his midriff.

"Come on in here, boy," he called when he saw them enter. He did not bother to get up. "What are you doing out here this time of night?"

Pete took a chair near Mr. Kelly, leaving Jan standing rather uncomfortably near the door.

"Is this the pretty girl you have been telling me about?"

"Yes, sir," Pete replied, "this is Jan Edwards."

"Well, come on in here, Jan Edwards, and have a seat. Pete tells me that he couldn't have pulled off this moon rock thing without you."

Jan, a bit awed at the spacious room and expensive furniture, sat on an ottoman near Pete's chair. Mr. Kelly gave her a slow, appraising look, then turned back to Pete.

"What's on your mind, Pete boy?" he asked.

"Well, nothing, I hope, but I caught a couple of boys playing around the old Meeks pier."

"Who?" Mr. Kelly asked sharply.

"Just a couple of ninth-graders. One was the Ta kid and the other was Joseph Boyd."

Mr. Kelly picked up his beer can, took the last swallow, and set the can back on the table thoughtfully.

"That Ta kid, huh," he muttered. "Did they go out there?"

"Nah, I'm sure they didn't. The only thing that bothers me is that I found a scrap of that jacket on the shore."

"What jacket?"

"The one we took to wrap the rock in."

"Did the boys see it?"

"I'm not sure. It was under the bluff."

"Did you talk to them?"

"Yeah, I warned them not to fool around there anymore."

"What did they say?"

"Nothing. They just left."

"Did you check the rock?"

"Yeah. I waded out there and it is right where I left it. Do you think I ought to move it, Mr. Kelly?"

Mr. Kelly picked up the empty beer can, shook it, and set it back on the table. He leaned over the arm of his chair and shouted toward the open doorway.

"Juan, bring us a couple of beers in here." He turned back to Jan. "You want anything to drink, little lady?" he asked.

Jan shook her head.

"My wife has probably got some sodas or tea or something in there."

"No, thank you." Jan shifted her position on the stool. She wondered if they should be discussing the moon rock, if Juan lurked near enough to hear Mr. Kelly's shout. How many people knew about this, anyway? Maybe the noise from the television was enough to muffle their discussion. Mr. Kelly seemed to have become conscious of the television at the same moment, for his eyes went back to the basketball game.

"That is the sorriest bunch of players I ever saw," he remarked to Pete. "Look at 'em. That's the third time that bean-pole, son-of-a-gun from New York has stolen the ball."

After Juan had served the beer and left the room, Mr. Kelly turned back to Pete.

"No, I don't think there is any reason to move it, Pete. I don't know of any place it would be any safer. The police are snooping around everywhere. The county sheriff has his nose in it now. Even that federal investigator was in my office this morning."

Jan felt a chill of fear. "Oh, what did he want?" she asked.

Mr. Kelly did not appear to be concerned. "He just asked a lot of questions. He asked about my boys on the dock. He doesn't know anything. Mostly, he just wanted my cooperation. I don't think we have anything to worry about."

"What about the boys?" Pete asked.

"Watch 'em. Watch the pier. If you think they may be going out there, stop 'em. I hope it won't come to that, but if they do actually find out about the rock, I'll have to turn them over to Eric."

"Eric?" Jan's question was almost involuntary. "Who is Eric?"

"You just don't worry about that, little lady." Mr. Kelly's eyes had hardened. He had suddenly changed from the "good-old-boy" type to something that Jan did not like. "You just worry about gettin' you some pretty clothes to make that trip to England that I am sending you on. You wanted to see the Wimbledon tennis matches . . . you're goin' to see 'em. That is all you need to worry about."

"But —" Jan started to protest, but Mr. Kelly did not allow her to continue.

"Listen, little lady," he said, his glinty eyes never leaving her face, "Eric is a man that you do not want to meet. And you won't meet him, if you let me and Pete run this business here. The rock will be gone day after tomorrow, and then it will all be over. So you just keep your cool now. You've done your part. Understand?"

Jan did understand. The threat was absolutely clear. She looked at Pete, but his eyes were focused on the television screen. He would not look at her. A lump rose in her throat. In her lap, her hands were clenched so tightly that the knuckles showed white. She took a deep breath in an effort to calm her fears.

"Yes, I understand," she replied weakly.

"Good. Now, Pete, do you understand the plans for Sunday?"

"Yes, sir." Pete looked back at Mr. Kelly. "I pick up the rock sometime Saturday night or early Sunday morning. I put it on your boat, get in line with the others that are going to pass in front of the priest for his blessing, and after that, head for Roll Over Pass."

"Right. Señor Martinez's yacht will be out in the gulf, but one of his men will be fishing there on the west end of the bridge. He will have a big blue ice chest by his side. You are to put the rock in the blue ice chest on my boat and take it with you when you go to fish beside him. He will simply pick up the wrong chest and leave. After that, we are through with it."

"How about the money?"

"It will be in his ice chest. That is the one you bring home with you."

"Do you trust this man? Should I look to be sure the money is there?"

"You can trust him. I have gotten a couple of treasures for him before. The crazy fool has more money than sense. He just sits up there on that mountain of his and hoards these things he calls treasures. I was there once. The place is a regular museum. I don't know why he wants it all. Since most of it is stolen and smuggled in, he can't even invite many people up to see it."

"Yeah, I wondered about that," Pete said. "He sure can't let anyone know he's got a moon rock."

"Oh, yeah, there will be a few others as crazy as he is that he will show it to. I don't know what it is with these guys. Whatever it is, I don't see much sense in letting this opportunity pass to pick up a little extra change, huh?"

"No, sir," Pete agreed. "I can't see anything wrong with that."

Suddenly, Mr. Kelly threw back his head and laughed. "Just like the old days, Pete boy," he said, chuckling, "that's how Roll Over Pass got its name. After the government put the big tax on all the liquor that came into the port of Galveston, my great-granddaddy used to meet the boats coming down from New York or across from Europe right there at Roll Over Pass. They would roll their barrels of rum right across that narrow strip of land, and Granddaddy would pick them up and bring them across the bay right here to this house. Yes, sir, my great-granddaddy was quite a boy in his day."

Jan cringed. It seemed that the great-grandson was "quite a boy" too.

8

Joseph could see that something had gone wrong before he ever reached Huy. He saw him standing at the fountain in front of the school's main entrance. His whole body reflected an attitude of defeat. He stood with shoulders slumped and eyes downcast. Joseph hurried toward him.

"It happened," Huy said as Joseph approached. "Someone set a fire on the boat last night."

"Oh, Huy," Joseph said, "how bad?"

"Just a small one, but it was deliberately set."

"Did it do much damage?"

"No, it was set in a barrel. But it's my warning. Just like the break-in of your mother's car was yours!"

Joseph kicked the side of the fountain. He felt tears of helplessness and anger fill his eyes.

"That creep!" he said, brushing them away quickly. "He knows he's got us now. He knows that we can't tell, either."

"But he doesn't even know that we found the rock," Huy protested. "He can't know. We were already back before they drove up. And if he checked, the rock was just where he left it."

"Yeah, but he suspects. He has to suspect. Why else would he have done these things?" In the face of Huy's logical reasoning, Joseph brought his anger under control. "It just makes me feel so . . . so . . . ."

"Helpless?" Huy suggested. "I know. I feel the same way."

"Yeah, but it makes me mad too!"

"And hurts?"

"Yeah. I can't believe that Jan is messed up in this thing. I can't believe that we have put our families in danger. What can we do?"

"I don't know right now, but we'll have to think of something." Huy nodded his head toward the parking lot. "Let's get inside," he said. "Here comes Pierce. The less we're seen with him right now, the better."

As Joseph turned, he saw Miss Duncan and Mr. Pierce coming toward them. Mr. Pierce carried a large box with what appeared to be poster board sticking out of the top. They were laughing. Miss Duncan raised her hand as if to catch Joseph's attention, but Joseph looked quickly in another direction and followed Huy into the building.

Joseph could not concentrate during any of his classes. His mind kept going around and around, trying to think of a solution to his problem. If they told Mr. Pierce now — even if they could convince him that he and Huy were not involved — there was still Jan. She was certainly involved. Surely Pete had just used her, and she, unknowingly, had allowed it. In Joseph's mind, Pete was still the only criminal. But could Jan convince Mr. Pierce of this? Something must be done quickly, before Pete had time to harm Joseph's mother or Mr. Ta's boat.

He could think of only one solution: get the rock back to Pierce without anyone knowing who did it. But even this did not solve the problem. What would Pete do when he found the rock missing? Would he know that Joseph had taken it? He didn't know anything now. He only suspected.

Joseph was back where he started. He had to work out a very careful plan.

When he entered the library at sixth period, Joseph felt just as far away from a solution as he had at first period. He glanced toward the conference room. Mr. Pierce sat talking with a student. Joseph hoped that he would stay there. He had dreaded all day having to see him. It would be hard to avoid a conversation if they were both in the same room.

Miss Duncan smiled as Joseph walked into the office. "Hello," she said. "I have saved a job for you. I think we ought to take down the astronaut display. Would you clear that table and put up some of these things that I brought about oceanography?" She pointed to the box that Joseph had seen Mr. Pierce carrying that morning. "I thought that we could call it 'The Seven Seas.' You have such a good eye for display. Just choose whatever you like. You can find everything from Popeye the Sailor to Jacques Cousteau in there. You'll have no problem finding books to put with it."

"Yes, ma'am." Joseph hung up his jacket and walked over to the box.

"Is anything wrong, Joseph?" Miss Duncan asked.

"No, ma'am. Why?" For some reason, Joseph felt uncomfortable under her penetrating gaze.

"Oh, you just don't seem your usual cheerful self. Don't you feel well?"

"I'm okay. Hasn't Huy come in yet?" Joseph wanted to change the subject.

"Right on time," she answered, smiling at Huy as he entered the door. "After he files the book cards and puts up a few magazines, he can help you with the display."

"Good afternoon, Miss Duncan," Huy said politely. "Are you speaking of me?"

"Yes, we are. How are you, Huy?"

"Fine, thank you. I will get to those book cards now."

Miss Duncan frowned thoughtfully, glanced at both boys, and went back to her work at the typewriter.

Joseph picked up the box of materials for the display and took it to the table where the astronauts' pictures and biographies sat. He stared at each picture intently and then at the vacant place where the moon rock and the soil samples had been.

That was it! What if he could get the moon rock and simply put it back in its place? If he were careful, no one would know how it got back. No one would really care, either; and, more importantly, no one would question Jan. It was better than mailing it back as Mr. Wilhelm had hinted. Joseph had already thought of that, but in Kelly's Landing, the postmistress knew everyone. She would certainly suspect a package addressed to NASA. Yes, this was the best plan. How could it be done?

A picture of Miss Duncan's key ring tossed carelessly among the papers and books on her desk rose to Joseph's mind. Besides the library keys, various supply cabinet keys and her desk key, she also had a key to a side door of the school. She often misplaced her keys. He had helped several times in a frantic search for them when supplies were needed. Yes, he thought he had a plan, one that would work. But he must be careful.

Joseph picked up the box containing the oceanography materials and carried it back to Miss Duncan's office.

Miss Duncan looked up when he entered. "Problem?" she asked.

"No, not really. I was just thinking . . ." Joseph hesitated.

"That, sometimes, is a problem," Miss Duncan laughed. "What were you thinking?"

"Well, about this display. I was just thinking it might be better to leave the other one up. That is . . . uh, well, until all of this moon rock-theft business is all settled."

"Oh? Why?"

"Well . . . uh . . . I was just thinking that it would

keep reminding everyone about the theft . . . and maybe
. . . uh . . . maybe whoever took it would want to bring it
back." Joseph wished he had not said the last sentence.
Now, if he did bring it back, Miss Duncan would remember what he had said. Then again, she might just think
his idea had worked. He knew that Miss Duncan liked
him, and she would never suspect him of stealing.

He looked at her desk. There lay the keys half hidden by a stack of file folders. Joseph blushed just at the
thought that he might soon betray that trust. "I don't
know," he said uncertainly, "it was just an idea."

Miss Duncan nodded her head thoughtfully. "Okay,"
she said. "It is Friday, anyway. We'll leave it until next
week. We'll see what happens over the weekend."

Joseph put the box down on the floor beside the door.
Good! Over the weekend was long enough. His mother
would work until 11:00 tonight, but would be off Saturday and Sunday nights. She liked to sleep late on her off-
days, and everyone would be down at the docks on Sunday to watch the Blessing of the Fleet. If he could get the
rock before then, he could slip it back into the library
while all the townspeople watched the ceremonies.
Should he try it in the daylight? He needed to think
about that later. He just had to get the keys now.

The phone rang.

"Hello," Miss Duncan picked it up. She paused.
"Yes," she continued. "I think that I have that address
right here." She leaned over and began thumbing
through the file folders in her bottom drawer.

Almost of its own accord, Joseph's hand went out and
covered the keys lying on the desk. He squeezed them
tightly so that they would make no sound and slipped
them into his pocket.

"Yes, here it is." Miss Duncan began reading an address into the phone. Joseph turned quickly and left the
office. He hurried to the A-V room. After he checked to
make sure no one had gone in, he entered. He leaned
against the wall and took several deep breaths. His heart

raced and his knees felt rubbery. This role of a thief is not for me, he thought wryly. He would need to get himself under better control if he intended to carry out the rest of his plan. He took another deep breath, walked to a book truck piled high with returned films, and began putting them in order on the slanted shelves.

"Busy? Need any help?" It was Mr. Pierce's voice. Joseph looked around to see him standing in the door.

"No, it's okay. I'm just finishing up," Joseph answered.

"Going to take Lonesome for a walk this afternoon?"

"No, sir. I don't think so."

"Oh, too bad. I wanted to wrangle an invitation to go with you again."

"Sorry." Joseph turned back to his shelving.

Mr. Pierce stood in the doorway a moment, then turned and left the A-V room.

Joseph knew that he should have been more friendly to Mr. Pierce. He was a nice guy. Well, he would make it up to him after this weekend. He just could not afford to be too friendly right now. When he returned the rock, without Jan and Pete's involvement being exposed, then Pete would have no reason to carry out his threats. Besides, even Pete would not know who returned it. Nobody would know, not even Huy. He had to keep Huy out of it. He would work alone. To get away from Huy and Lonesome would take some doing, but late at night, he could do it.

He looked at his hands and saw that they trembled. He slipped the last film into its place and rubbed his hands together. Don't think about it anymore right now, he told himself. He walked out of the reading room.

The first person that he saw was Jan, seated at the *Reader's Guide* table, idly flipping the pages of one of the indexes. She motioned for him to come.

"Sit down," she whispered as he came up, "and pretend that you are helping me with this thing."

Joseph straddled the stool beside her.

"I just wanted to apologize for the way Pete acted last night," she said.

"It wasn't your fault," Joseph mumbled, taking the index from her and staring at the page. He could not trust himself to look at her.

"I know, but I want to apologize anyway." She paused. "And, Joseph, I want to ask you to stay away from that place. Pete can be mean sometimes."

"Yeah." Joseph wondered if she knew about his mother's car and the fire on Mr. Ta's boat. "Yeah," he repeated, "I do know. What was eating him last night? What's so special about that place, anyway? Why is he so mad?"

Jan shrugged. "I don't know. He is just like that at times. Anyway, it would be better if you just didn't cross him, okay?"

"Yeah, I guess." Joseph felt sure that Pete had put Jan up to having this talk with him. Pete was just using Jan to keep them away from the old store. This probably meant that he had not yet moved the rock.

"Jan," Joseph looked at her now, "why . . . why do you fool around with that guy? You know that you could have any boy in the school."

Jan reached out her hand and put it over Joseph's arm. "Thank you, Joseph," she said. "I don't really know why I go with him. Maybe, after this, I won't."

"After what?"

"Oh, I don't know . . . maybe after this weekend."

Joseph stood up quickly, pulling his arm from beneath her hand.

"Yeah," he said. "That would be good. I've got to get busy now. See ya."

The next time he looked, Jan had left the table and evidently had gone back to her classroom. The hour dragged on. He did his jobs routinely, trying not to think. This, of course, was impossible.

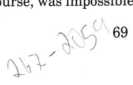

69

The dismissal bell had never sounded better than today. And Joseph had never felt more conscious of anything than what was in his pocket today. The keys pressed against his skin. Surely Miss Duncan would notice. He looked down. No, it was hardly noticeable. He went to the office to get his books and jacket.

9

Joseph and Huy managed to slip out of the library before Mr. Pierce had finished talking to the last student in the conference room.

"I saw Mr. Pierce go into the A-V room while you were there. What did he want?" asked Huy.

"He wanted to come with us this afternoon, but I didn't ask him. I don't think we need to be seen talking to him right now."

"Well, what did Jan want?" Huy asked. "Do you think that she is spying on us for Pete?"

"Maybe," Joseph shrugged. "I don't know. All she said was that we ought to be careful. I really don't understand her."

"Perhaps it is that you do not want to understand her."

"You're probably right."

As they approached the Ta boat, Lonesome leaped from his coiled rope bed and bounded toward the boys. Mr. Ta also seemed eager to see them. He stepped across the gangplank to the dock and began to speak before his usual bow.

"The police were here," he said. "They searched everywhere, in the house and on the boat. Do you think that Mr. Pierce did not believe us yesterday, my son?"

"Yes, Father, I think that he believed us. Perhaps the search was just routine."

"Do you think they searched my place?" Joseph broke in. "I'm going to run up to the restaurant and call my mom."

This might be the solution that Joseph sought. If the police had already searched, then it would be safe to store the rock at home until he could get it back to the library. He hurried up the steps of the restaurant.

"Yes," his mother said, when he had gotten her on the phone, "they were there this morning, but don't worry about it, baby. The nice officer said that it was more to free you of suspicion than to implicate you."

That settles it, Joseph thought, as he hung up. He was surprised how smoothly things were falling into place. If he got the rock tonight, he could take it home with him, unless he could find a good hiding place near the school. He would need to leave Huy's early in order to look around the campus on his way home.

It had been hard to tell Huy the small lie about homework. Twice, in the same day, Joseph had committed a deliberate sin. He consoled himself that keeping Huy out of his plan was safer for the Ta family. As for the keys in his pocket, he would return them and it would hurt no one.

He walked quickly along the wharf, past the other shrimp boats, and headed for the school.

The late norther had pushed its way through Kelly's Landing and a warm, humid south wind billowed the sails of a few pleasure boats out in the bay. The sun was warm, but Joseph knew that the breeze might turn chilly again at night. The tide would be high too. Except for a fleeting thought of undertow, this did not worry him. He had boated and swum these bay waters since he was eight years old. The fact was that he could not choose his time to go get the rock. He must do it after dark and before his mother got home at 11:00. He realized he was about to break every water safety rule in the book, but he was a strong swimmer and would take no unnecessary chances.

As he circled the campus looking for a safe place to hide the rock until Sunday morning, he spotted the weedy culvert where he had first found Lonesome. He paused at the overgrown ditch which completely hid the end of concrete pipe. Why not? Lonesome had been hard enough to see, and he had wallowed the grass down in front of the opening. Now the grass hid it again. It was on the same side of the building as the door that Miss Duncan's key fit. No one would see it here.

He left, satisfied that he had found the perfect hiding place.

At 8:30, Joseph prepared to leave. He had two and a half hours before his mother would get home. Wearing jeans and a sweatshirt over his swim suit, he screwed his luggage carrier onto his bike. Then he pedaled to the jetty.

He had decided to enter the water from the end of the jetty. The swim would be longer, but he knew he could not get into the water closer to the pier, because of Pete; nor could he enter the water close to the Ta boat, because of Lonesome.

Joseph propped his bike on the sheltered side of the boulders, skinned off his shoes, jeans, and sweatshirt, and headed for the end of the jetty. He knew that getting into the water would be more dangerous here. The rocks were slick and there was likely to be an undertow since the tide had come in. He could not think about that now. It would take too long to wade and swim out from the shore.

As he made his way across the wet boulders in the semi-darkness, goose bumps covered his body. He shuddered and moved as quickly as he could. His eyes became accustomed to the faint red glow reflected from the rocks. Lights strung along the big pipes and holding tanks of the nearby oil refineries illuminated the night sky along this part of the bay. The rising full moon added to the eerie light.

The water felt warm as Joseph slid into it. He reached for the bottom with his toes, but discovered the tide was already too high. He began an easy dog-paddle toward the silhouette of the old Meeks pier.

Joseph had always loved the ethereal feeling of half-floating, half-swimming on the rising and falling surf. The rhythm of the waves hypnotized him into a state of calm and confidence. He was amazed that on such a dangerous mission he could remain so composed. He remembered how upset and frightened he was after taking Miss Duncan's keys. Now, moving toward a pier in the dark, planning to retrieve a priceless national treasure, he had no such feelings.

When he reached the pier, the level of the water came to just below the trap door of the old Meeks store. He clung to the ladder and pushed the trap door inward. As he emerged from the water, he gasped. The cold wind on his wet skin set his teeth to chattering.

Quickly, he climbed up into the room and found the moon rock behind the counter. He tied the strings of the duffel bag about his waist. He wondered about Huy's jacket. It might be useful as a disguise when he strapped the duffel bag onto his bike. He untied the strings and stuffed the jacket into the bag with the rock. Anxious to be back in the warm water, he hurriedly retied the strings about his waist and dropped himself through the trap door.

Clinging to the ladder under the pier, waves crashed into Joseph in quick succession. The water level had risen sharply in the short time that he was in the store. Simultaneously, he thought "rip current" and felt his feet leave the rung of the ladder. The heavy, wet duffel bag jerked at his waist. He lost his grip and somersaulted downward, out of control. He felt his body being swept out to sea by the strong undertow.

As he fought to pull himself up to the surface, the current dragged him further down. Finally, he felt the bottom. He managed to get his feet under him and sprang upward. After what seemed a lifetime, his face broke the surface and he inhaled hungrily. He gagged on the salt water he had swallowed. His nose and eyes burned and his chest ached.

Treading water furiously, he looked for the shore. He must not swim toward the shore or the current would catch him again. He must not lose his head. He must not let this current beat him. Fighting against the tremendous drag, he flailed his arms and legs, struggling to gain a few yards away from the current. Finally, he felt the pull lessen and then stop. A few more strokes and he turned on his back and floated. He breathed deeply and rested.

Gradually, the muscles in his arms and legs relaxed. Relief swept over him. He had won. Conscious of the duffel bag at his waist, he put down his hand and felt the lucite lump still safely inside. His job was not finished. A few more minutes of rest and he must get the rock to its hiding place. He rolled over on his stomach to get his bearing and was surprised to find how far out he had drifted. He located the pier and the jetty. Now out of the rip current, the waves would help push him toward the shore.

Just as he started to turn toward the jetty, car lights bouncing along the bluff above the pier caught his eye. The car stopped and the lights went out. Pete! What if Pete went out to check the rock? Surely he wouldn't now, with the tide at its peak. Surely he would wait until it went back out. Joseph began swimming in long, lazy strokes. Don't rush now, he told himself. Don't tire out. Take it easy. Take it easy.

Too exhausted to try to climb the jetty's slick rocks, he swam until he could touch bottom. He hardly noticed the cold or the fog which had begun to roll in as he pulled on his jeans and sweatshirt. He strapped the duffel bag and coat to his bike.

Joseph saw no one as he pedaled up the sloped road and onto the flat street. He circled the school campus. The city police had always kept a routine watch around the school at night, but he feared that they might have stepped up the security even more since the robbery. The campus appeared deserted, and he saw no patrol car. When he came to the culvert the second time, he stopped. It took only a few seconds to unstrap the bag and shove it inside the concrete pipe. He made sure that the grass still covered the hole before he mounted his bike again and started home.

10

The following morning, Joseph waked early. He lifted his arms to stretch and felt a grip of pain in his shoulders. Swimming each day in the school pool had not prepared his muscles for the fight against the undertow last night.

He ran his fingers gingerly around his waist. A red whelp marked the place where the rope had burned him. He had not known about the burn nor the long scrape on his leg until he had undressed for bed. Throwing back the sheet, he examined his leg. Small pockets of white infection rose along a red path where barnacles had cut and scraped the skin.

He looked at the clock. It was 7:00. He had promised to be at the Ta boat by 8:00 to help decorate it. Stifling a groan, he rolled out of bed.

Joseph planned to put some first-aid cream on his leg and slip out to eat breakfast. He knew that his mother would sleep late. Lifting his arms, he forced them into wide, swinging circles — first forward, then backward. After the first few moments of torture, the muscles began to relax and the stiffness to disappear. He dressed and left the apartment quietly.

Joseph hoped that his breakfast at a fast-food restaurant was not an indication of how the rest of his day would go. As he started to the table with his loaded tray, he slipped, spilling his orange juice on his hot, fluffy biscuit. He grabbed for some extra napkins on the counter and managed to upset the napkin holder. The holder slid and upset a container of straws. The straws spilled and upset the sleepy young woman behind the cash register.

"Sorry," he offered meekly and made his way to a table.

The food made him feel better. The terrible fear that had engulfed him, as the undertow grabbed him, had left. A person could never be sure how he would react to danger until he was faced with it. Joseph was pleased with himself that he had not given way to panic. The rock was in a safe place. If he continued to keep his head and be careful, it would all be over tomorrow.

These comforting thoughts were interrupted when Pete Hebert pushed open the door. Pete's eyes swept the room and came to rest on Joseph. He hunched his shoulders and sauntered toward Joseph's table. His tousled hair, wrinkled clothes, and red-rimmed eyes suggested a lack of sleep. Joseph wondered if Jan had been with him on the bluff last night.

"Where's your good buddy?" Pete growled, as he approached the table.

"Who?" Joseph asked innocently.

"You know who," Pete scowled, "your 'Nam buddy."

"Home, I guess." Joseph looked back at his plate. "Why?"

"Why? Because, I just want to be sure that he is not out runnin' up and down the water's edge, that's why. I heard that his boat almost caught fire night before last. Is that right?"

Resentment and anger overcame his initial dread at seeing Pete. He looked up. "You know it did," he said, looking directly at Pete's face. "You also know what happened to my mother's car."

"That's right, I sure do. But you'll have a hard time proving it."

Joseph looked back down at his plate. A feeling of relief swept over him as soon as he realized that Pete did not know the rock was gone. Suddenly, his soggy breakfast tasted better. He even managed a slight smile as Pete turned from the table.

Joseph finished his breakfast and headed for the dock.

Huy and Lonesome stood waiting for Joseph when he came into sight. Less patient than Huy, Lonesome pounced onto the dock, circling and barking, impeding, rather than hastening, Joseph's arrival.

"Mother and Father are not quite ready to begin decorating," Huy said. "Let's go work off some of Lonesome's energy."

"Good," agreed Joseph.

Without consulting each other, both turned in the opposite direction from the Meeks pier.

"How did the studying go last night?" Huy asked tentatively.

Joseph felt the same hesitation that he had felt yesterday about lying to Huy. In order to avoid answering, he walked a few steps to where a pile of driftwood had collected in a small cove. As he stooped over to select a stick, a larger piece dislodged and rolled against his leg. Involuntarily, he winced and drew in his breath. His leg hurt badly.

"What's the matter," Huy asked. "Did you hurt yourself?"

"A little," Joseph answered, running his hand down the leg of his pants.

"Let's see."

"Nah, it's okay," Joseph said, limping in spite of his effort to walk normally.

"Let me look," Huy persisted.

Joseph hurled the stick.

"Fetch," he commanded Lonesome.

79

When Lonesome had retrieved the stick and received his praise, Joseph looked back at Huy. Huy stood motionless with a bewildered expression on his face.

"Why are you looking at me like that?" Joseph asked.

"I am surprised, that's all. What has happened since yesterday? You avoided my company then, and now you are avoiding my questions."

Joseph squirmed under the steady gaze. He could stand the deception no longer.

"If I tell you something," he began, hesitantly, "will you try to understand why I left you out of my plans?"

"That depends on what the plans were. But, yes, I'll try to understand."

Joseph took a deep breath and began his story. He told Huy everything that had transpired from the time he had first conceived of the idea of returning the rock through his last conversation with Pete a few moments earlier. There was a long silence when he finished.

Huy shook his head in disbelief.

"Alone . . . you have done all of this alone? I am grateful, Joseph, but what if something had happened to you? You should have told me, at least."

"I know," he said quietly, "I'm sorry."

Huy questioned Joseph about his plan for placing the rock back into the library. He offered to help, but Joseph still felt that there would be less risk if he worked alone.

"I've got it all thought out, Huy. Let me finish it. I'll come over just as soon as I put it back."

"Well, that can be as early as you like, because I have to watch the boat while my parents and sisters go to early mass."

"Then I'll come straight here."

"Good."

The boys turned back after this agreement and returned to the boat with very little conversation between them, each deep in thought.

"Hi, boys." They heard a shout. It was Pierce. He

waved from the deck of Mr. Ta's boat. Huy and Joseph looked at each other warningly, but simultaneously waved back just as if nothing troubled them. Both boys felt that they had become pretty good at keeping a secret.

As they neared the boat, they saw Vince helping Mr. Ta put the try net back in its regular position. Mrs. Ta stood to the side, giving instructions.

"What's going on?" Joseph asked lightly.

"Mrs. Ta has changed her decorating scheme. She wants the try net back to the side where it belongs," answered Mr. Ta.

Joseph and Huy greeted Vince and began to get in on the new plan for the decorations. As they gathered the necessary pliers, scissors, wire, tape, streamers, flags and flowers to work with, they listened as Vince asked Mr. Ta question after question about his boat, his crew, his schedule, and even his financing.

Mr. Ta was pleased with Vince's genuine interest as he answered each one.

"As the captain, I navigate my boat to the spot of my choosing — sometimes in sight of land, sometimes beyond. Most of the time, I sail with several other Vietnamese boats. We agree on an area and pilot together. The Americans prefer to sail independently, for the most part, but we generally sail in a cluster."

"Do you help other shrimpers get started financially?" Vince asked.

"Yes, we help each other in many ways. Sometimes, before we have funds enough to obtain our own craft, we hire out as a captain of another owner's boat."

"Does the captain have to fill in on the other crewmen's jobs?"

"Oh, yes, if necessary. We oversee the harvesting of the catch from all angles, from the first dropping of the try net to the icing down of the headed shrimp."

"You seem to enjoy your work," said Vince.

Mr. Ta nodded. "I do. I enjoy owning my own boat. It requires many decisions, but it is good. I have been the header and the rigger before. Both jobs are very hard and require great strength and endurance."

"What does the header do?" asked Vince.

Mr. Ta grinned. "He heads — but first, he gets ready. Just as soon as the rigger hauls in the nets and unloosens that bag knot, every imaginable object from the ocean's floor is dumped on the deck. The header sorts it out with great care. His white boots become his battle armor at that time because the net gathers in jellyfish, crabs, poisonous squirrel fish, glass, metal, and much more. At times, the seaweed snarls this debris together and the sorting is a gruesome chore."

"It sounds dangerous."

"It is."

"Boy, I'll say," chimed in Joseph. "Your hands get to be a mess, all cut up. And you get yellow 'gunk' on your hands that won't come off."

"Oh?" Vince's eyebrows went up.

"What Joseph is talking about is what we call 'shrimp poisoning.' It comes from an acid that comes out of the little lances on the sides of the shrimp. Even with thick gloves, the lances pierce through, at times, and the poison is released. The header's fingers smell badly and become stained. Most headers have yellow hands, even if they are not Oriental." Mr. Ta laughed at his own joke.

"But it peels off, finally," Joseph added.

"What incentive is there to be a header?" Vince quizzed.

Mr. Ta thought a moment, then answered. "Money. A good, fast header can sort, separate the heads from the tails, pack them in ice, and be ready for the next drag of the net. The faster the harvesting goes, the faster the marketing goes. The rigger knows just when to haul up the next load by watching the header's progress."

"What is the rigger doing while the header 'heads'?"

"He just starts over. All of the net operations are his, the dragging, the hoisting, lowering the outriggers, the stabilizers, the net doors, and the mending of the net if it tears. And, also, he's the cook. He is the only one with a bit of time in between hauls. He prepares the food and we eat it without stopping our work. Once we start a haul, we are committed to it and it lasts all day into the night, or all night into the day." Mr. Ta continued to point out and explain each mechanism during their conversation.

"Do you shrimp in the same place, usually?"

Joseph and Huy both giggled. They couldn't believe that Vince could be that uninformed. Mr. Ta answered patiently.

"No, they migrate from day to day in huge schools. Actually, they hide from us, but we keep looking until we find them."

"What do you do when you are short-handed?"

"I have taken the boys out at times." He looked at them fondly. "They work very hard, but their hearts are not in it. They will not become shrimpers, I feel."

Huy teased his father. "We shall become shrimp-boat exterior decorators."

Joseph began to relax somewhat with the preparation of the fleet festivities as he and Huy taped flowers to the rigging. The pain of his waist and leg reminded him of the problem at hand, but he did feel less uncomfortable around Vince with the Ta family present. He waved to a man on another shrimper and then called back to Vince.

"Do you want to go and meet the King of the Fleet?"

"Sure." Vince walked toward Joseph enthusiastically. Joseph could tell that Vince was enjoying himself.

On the short walk to the captain's inlet, Vince commented to Joseph about not seeing him much lately. Joseph was glad that it was a short walk. He did not want to get involved in that subject right now.

Clevens Richard worked alone on his boat, which was docked in a recessed area with a singular pier space. He studied the pair as Vince and Joseph neared his streamer-adorned vessel. Anyone could guess that Captain Richard's rigging wore a badge of rank.

Joseph greeted him warmly and introduced the two men, glad for someone else with whom Vince could talk.

In the course of their conversation, Vince found out that tomorrow, Captain Clevens Richard would again wear the crown and the robe and carry the trophy of the King of the Fleet, an honor reserved for the oldest shrimper who still shrimped. However, at the moment, the captain did not look much like a king.

He wore raveled cut-offs and a sleeveless shirt, unbuttoned to midchest, exposing thick, white chest hair. He had on the ever-present white boots, to keep his feet cooler, but he wore no cap over his heavy mat of white hair to protect him from the sun. His tan was bean-brown. Around his neck he wore a gold medallion that was presented to him last year as "King." The medallion symbolized the Savior. A ship's wheel formed the background. Christ, with arms extended, hung from the spokes. His feet rested on the top of the post of a traditional anchor. The medallion hung from a corded golden chain.

The men talked about ten minutes, with Vince asking a question about every thirty seconds. Joseph wondered if he ever stopped. He was glad that he was asking someone else the questions, though, instead of him. Joseph saw Huy coming and felt relieved. He had dreaded the walk back to the boat with Pierce alone.

After the three wished Captain Richard a happy day for tomorrow, they went back to the Ta boat. Just as they stepped on deck, Joseph stumbled and went down on his injured leg. He got up quickly, but he saw Vince watching him. He wondered if Vince had noticed his pained expression.

"Looks as if two someones I know stayed up too late last night watching TV." He reached over to touch Joseph on the shoulder, but Joseph drew away.

Mr. Ta, having seen Joseph fall, came toward the group and heard Vince's remark. "The boys were not together last night."

"Oh?" Vince again used his one-word question.

Huy answered a bit too excitedly. "Joseph had homework, and I helped my mother with the paper flowers."

"I see."

Joseph knew that Vince did not believe a word of it, but there was no turning back now. He had to go through with his plan. He looked at Vince as he tried to be cool. "Are you going to be around later?" he asked.

"Why do you ask?"

Joseph became exasperated. "Do you ask questions all of the time?"

Vince laughed. "You just asked one." He laughed again. "In answer to your question — no, I won't be around later. I am taking your librarian out to dinner. In fact, I need to leave right now. I have some business to tend to before we go out."

Vince said his goodbyes to all and left.

"Why did you ask him if he would be around later?" Huy asked Joseph.

"I really don't know. I just couldn't think of anything else to say right then. I'm glad he's gone."

"Me too. I think."

"Yeah, me too . . . I think."

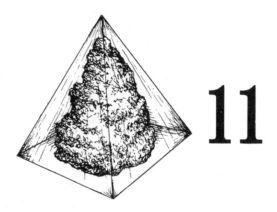

11

Joseph could not get to sleep. It was almost 1:00 A.M. His mother was off for the weekend, and they had gone to bed early. He had played his radio until his mother came in at midnight and asked him to turn it off. He had barely had time to cover his hurt leg and waist when she knocked, then opened the door.

The rope burn was better, but his leg still looked bad. He fished the first-aid cream from the drawer of his bedside table and gingerly applied another coating to the wounds. He tried again to concentrate on Benjamin Franklin's autobiography, which he was reading for English class. But as smart as the old guy was, Benjamin was no competition for the thoughts that kept crowding into Joseph's mind about what he must do in a few hours.

He had gone over it a hundred times. There really was nothing else to think about. At 1:30 he gave up on the book, snapped off his bed lamp, and slipped into a fretful sleep. He woke at 2:30, at 4:00, and again at 5:00.

At 5:30 it was light enough that he could claim to be going to Huy's boat if someone asked him.

The sun was not yet up, but the eastern sky was already turning silver. A milky, damp fog hung close to the ground, blurring the shapes of familiar houses, cars, and trees along the street.

As he unchained his bicycle from the post in his mother's parking space, he glanced overhead. Through the haze, he could barely make out a thin layer of cumulus clouds, generally associated with fair weather, moving across the sky from south to north. He knew the fog would lift soon; but now, as he rode into the deserted street, he welcomed its protection.

As he reached the main highway leading through town, the traffic signal turned yellow. He thought he heard the sound of a car motor as he stopped, but no one pulled up behind him. A truck and two cars, each pulling a boat trailer, passed slowly in front of him when the light changed to red. They were headed toward Galveston. Many people would gather early and vie for a good position in the water from which to watch the Blessing of the Fleet. The shore would also be crowded with spectators.

When the light turned green, Joseph crossed the highway and headed toward the school. A car materialized dimly in the fog ahead of him. He slowed down. The car was creeping along, slowing to a near stop at intervals. Each time it slowed, there was a dull thud along the sidewalk. Joseph decided that it was the *Houston Post* carrier. He stopped his bike until the car disappeared around the next corner into the fog.

He circled the school campus twice before stopping at the culvert to listen intently. There was no sound other than the lonely mourn of a tugboat foghorn somewhere out in the ship channel which ran through Galveston Bay. He felt a sudden surge of apprehension as he climbed down into the ditch and reached into the concrete pipe. It was still there. Quickly, he unwrapped Huy's coat from around it, worked loose the rope of the duffel bag, and pulled the rock from inside. He stuffed the bag and coat back into the culvert, made sure that the weeds covered the end, and started back up the incline of the ditch to his bike.

The roar of a car motor startled Joseph. Squealing tires on wet pavement came toward him and slid to a stop beside him. Joseph hugged the rock to his chest and, scooping his bike up from the wet grass, he pedaled as fast as he could across the campus and away from the road. He heard a car door slam and Pete's angry voice behind him.

"You won't get away with this. Stop now, before I have to kill you!" Pete shouted. "I have a gun! Stop now!"

Joseph did not even look back. In the first few minutes, fear had almost paralyzed his mind but not his body. He was passing the school building now with no thought except to get away from Pete.

He heard the car door slam a second time and the motor start. The sound jolted his thoughts back to reality. His only hope was to find someone, anyone, who could help him. He thought first of Vince Pierce, but he had no idea where he was staying. Why had he not asked? Why had he not told Vince the whole story yesterday?

The police were his next best bet. The station was only three blocks away. He cut across the tennis courts and headed for the street back of the school. When he reached the edge of the campus, he could not see Pete's car. He bounced off the curb and started toward the police station.

The motor sounded behind him and he looked over his shoulder. He could not see the car for a few seconds, then it lurched out of the fog. The minute Joseph saw Pete, Pete must have seen Joseph, for there was a grinding gear shift, a roar of the motor, and the car plunged directly toward him at top speed. Still clutching the moon rock in his left arm, Joseph jerked upward on the handlebar. The bike lurched dangerously to the side, but the front wheel cleared the curb, and Joseph was back across the sidewalk and into the grass and trees of the campus.

Pete's car hit the curb at the exact spot where Joseph had just been. It bounced back into the street and came to a spinning halt.

Joseph did not wait to see what happened next. He headed back across the tennis courts and around the school building. As he rounded the corner, he could not see the car. The fog was too thick.

Joseph knew now that he must stay off the streets. If the fog could cover him for a few minutes, he could cut across a vacant lot and get to an alley behind the buildings which lined the wharf. Surely someone would be up and out along the waterfront. Pete couldn't very well kill him in front of people. Adrenaline that fear had pumped into his bloodstream helped him to pedal faster, now that he knew where he was going. He was well across the street and into the vacant lot when he heard Pete's car again. The sound passed and faded in the opposite direction.

He reached the buildings along the wharf. The small space between two of them was crowded with old tires, oyster dredges, and crab traps. He had no idea what he intended to do now. He got off of his bike, worked his way through the clutter on foot, and stumbled onto the dock. He leaned against the building, gasping for breath.

"Is anyone here?" he called hoarsely. "Ahoy there! Is anyone on board?"

He waited, breathing deeply to steady his voice and calm his fear. He tried again.

"Ahoy there!" His voice was stronger. "Is anyone on board? Please, if you are there, please answer me."

He leaned against the building again. What was the word for "help" in Vietnamese? He wished that he had learned more of the language from Huy. He wished that he had told Mr. Pierce about the moon rock as soon as he and Huy had discovered it. He wished . . .

A dog barked in the distance. The barking grew nearer. Lonesome burst out of the mist and bounded toward him. Joseph let his body slide down the wall of the building and, with his free arm, hugged Lonesome around the neck.

"Good boy," he half sobbed, "but what are we going to do now?"

Lonesome wagged his tail and turned back toward the direction from which he had come.

"No, Lonesome," Joseph said, "we can't go to Huy's boat now."

"Why not?"

Joseph looked up and saw Huy standing only a few feet from him.

Huy stared at the rock. "Oh," he said, "you have it with you!"

"Oh, Huy!" Joseph cried. "Yes, and Pete is after me in his car. He nearly ran me down. He caught me taking it out of the culvert."

Huy was already pulling Joseph to his feet and urging him along the dock. "Then we must get to the boat," he said. "Come on. We can get out on the bay a little way, and I will call the sheriff on the radio."

"Good." Joseph felt a wave of relief sweep over him. "I hadn't thought of that. I was trying to get to the police station when Pete nearly hit me with his car."

The boys broke into a run, Lonesome leading the way.

Once on board, Joseph untied the rope which held them to the dock. Huy hurried to the pilot house and started the engine. The noise seemed deafening, amplified by the fog and the early-morning stillness. The boat began to move slowly out of its berth and through the narrow path between the other boats in the slip.

"How did you know where I was?" Joseph asked when they were safely into the bay. "Did you hear me call?"

"No," Huy replied, flipping on the fog lights and speeding up a bit. "I'm sure Lonesome did, though. When I got to the boat, instead of greeting me he took off down the dock, barking and running like mad. I just followed him."

"Wow! What a dog!" Joseph reached out and scratched behind Lonesome's ear. Then he frowned. "Should you have turned on the lights?" he asked. "Won't that make it easy for someone to see us?"

Huy laughed. "Of course," he said, "that is why I turned them on. I am about to call the sheriff, and we want him to see us. Besides, I certainly can't take a chance of wrecking my father's boat in this fog." Huy throttled the boat down to its slowest speed and reached for the radio microphone. Joseph put his hand over Huy's.

"Wait," he said. "Let's think a minute. Maybe we can still think of some way to get this rock back in the library."

Huy shook his head. "If you are thinking about Jan again, just forget it," he said firmly. "Jan is just going to have to face up to whatever comes. We all are!"

"Yeah." Joseph turned away and began patting Lonesome again. "I guess you're right."

Huy reached for the microphone again, but his hand stopped in midair.

"Listen," he said, holding one finger across his lips.

Over the throb of the shrimper's engine came the faint hum of a motorboat. The hum steadily increased in volume. The boys climbed down from the pilot house and onto the aft deck. A bright headlight bumped across the surface of the water toward them.

"It's Pete!" Joseph slapped his hand on the boat's rail angrily. "He saw me headed toward the wharf. Of course, he figured out exactly what I would do!"

"Right," Huy agreed. "No one else would be taking a chance like that in this fog." He ran back to the pilot house. Joseph followed.

"Speed it up," Joseph advised. "Try to get to some port where there are people."

The moon rock still sat on a stool where Joseph had

91

put it. He grabbed it and climbed down to the deck. He heard the engine rev and felt the wind increase against his face as the boat picked up speed.

Joseph knew what he was going to do. He lowered the try net and forced himself to remain calm as he carefully examined the sack knot that tied the bottom of the net together. There were six tight loops of rope. He pulled up one more so that the end of the rope would be too short to catch on some obstacle in the water. He dropped the moon rock into the net, swung the small, wooden doors outward, and lowered the net into the water. The doors would open the front end of the net and cause it to sink to the bottom.

The bouncing spotlight was only a short distance behind them now. Joseph could make out the shape of a speedboat and Pete behind the wheel. Pete lifted his arm and a pistol shot cracked above the roar of the motor. Joseph ducked behind the boat rail and crawled toward the pilot house.

"He has a pistol," Joseph said as he crawled into the cabin. "Can you outrun him?"

"No."

"What can we do?"

"I don't know. He will have to make the next move."

It did not take long for Pete to make that move. A shattering of glass startled them. Slivers from the window of the pilot house flew across the room and slid across the instrument panel in front of Huy. The speedboat came alongside of them and rapidly worked its way in front and across their path. Huy cut the engine.

"We'll have to stop," he said resignedly. "He'll wreck us if we don't. We had better get out on deck."

Lonesome, barking menacingly, circled the back deck as Pete nosed his boat up against the rear of the shrimper.

"Throw down a rope," Pete ordered gruffly. Lonesome reared, placing his front paws on the ship's rail. His lips curled back, exposing his teeth. A deep growl escaped from his throat. "And get that dog down in the hold, if you don't want him shot," Pete added.

Huy threw down the rope. Pete balanced himself precariously on the front of his boat and tied it to the shrimper. Joseph had an almost uncontrollable urge to do something to upset Pete's vessel, but he knew that it would only make Pete madder. Nothing short of killing Pete would do them any good now. Joseph urged Lonesome away from the rail and, as gently as possible, forced him to jump down into the hold.

"We'll just have to worry about getting you out later," he told Lonesome hopelessly.

At first, Lonesome seemed so surprised at what Joseph had forced him to do that he looked up and whimpered questioningly. Then, with a surge of energy, he began to leap as high as he could toward the opening above his head. Over and over, barking furiously, he leaped and fell back to the floor.

"No, Lonesome, no," Joseph commanded. "You'll hurt yourself. No! Quiet! No!" Joseph's voice was pleading.

"Very smart advice," Pete said. Joseph turned and found Pete standing directly behind him. " 'Cause if he doesn't calm down, I may have to calm him down with this." Pete's pistol pointed directly at Joseph's chest.

Joseph turned back to speak to Lonesome. "It's okay, boy. Quiet . . . Quiet . . . That's a good boy."

Lonesome quit barking and leaping but continued pacing the hold like a caged lion.

"Now," Pete said, when Joseph turned back to face him, "where is it?"

"What?" Joseph tried to look innocent.

"Come on, man, don't try to play games with me." Pete put the barrel of the gun against Joseph's chest. "Now, you want to tell me where it is?"

Joseph swallowed hard. What a fool he had been to think that he could hide the moon rock from Pete. He swallowed again.

"In the try net," he answered, nodding toward the side of the shrimper.

"Smart. Oh, very smart," Pete snarled. "Get it."

Joseph walked slowly to midship and started working the gears which hauled in the net. As he pulled on the long handle, a plan took shape in his mind. Maybe he could have one last chance. When the net appeared over the top of the rail, Joseph locked the gear handle and went to the side. As he reached to pull the net on board, he fumbled with it clumsily until he made sure that his hand found the end of the rope with the sack knot.

"Come on, come on," Pete ordered. "Get the thing on board."

"I'll help," Huy said, starting toward Joseph.

"No, Huy. I'm getting it," Joseph cried. "Here it comes, right now."

Joseph pushed the wet net as hard as he could toward Pete. At the same time, he held tightly to the end of the sack knot, feeling it unravel like the string on a sack of Lonesome's dog food. The end of the net opened up, spilling its contents all over Pete and the entire aft deck. Pete threw up his arms to protect his face from the shower of sea creatures and mud. He lost his balance on the slippery deck and fell. The gun dropped from his hand and slid into the hold with Lonesome.

"Wrap him in the net," Joseph called to Huy, but the order was unnecessary. Huy had already jumped into the slimy mess on top of Pete and was working the net over him. Pete fought and tried to stand up, but the more he flailed his arms, the more entangled he became in the net; and the more he tried to stand up, the farther down his body Huy was able to work the webbing. When the net reached Pete's feet, Huy hit hard at the back of Pete's knees. His knees buckled and Pete fell back on the muddy deck. Huy jerked the net over Pete's feet and began pulling the end of the net together again with the rope. Pete lay cursing and helpless among the flapping fish and crawling crabs.

94

"Thanks for the help," Huy said breathlessly as he gave the rope a final tug and tied the end.

"You didn't need any," Joseph replied in amazement. "I never saw anything like it."

"Really?" Huy stood up.

"Really." Joseph looked at Huy and covered his mouth with his hand to prevent Huy from seeing his smile. "In fact," he added, "I never saw anything like you."

Huy was covered with mud. It caked his thick, black hair and covered his face, almost obscuring his soft, dark eyes. His clothes clung wetly to his slender body, and a tiny crab hung relentlessly to one of his shoelaces.

Huy looked down at himself. "No, I don't guess you ever did," he said, grinning at Joseph. "I guess I know what those lady mud wrestlers feel like now."

Pete still struggled on the deck, promising to deal them every kind of misery worse than death if they did not let him out of the net.

Huy shrugged. "Did you find the moon rock in all of this mess?" he asked Joseph.

"I had forgotten all about it," Joseph gasped, horrified. He began to look around. "Yes, there it is, over by the rail. I can't believe that I hadn't even thought about it."

"It doesn't look like much of a priceless national treasure right now, does it?"

"Hardly," Joseph agreed. He looked up as he heard the unmistakable sound of a helicopter overhead. For the first time, he noticed that the sun was well up and that the fog had lifted. "Do you think they are looking for us?" Joseph asked.

"Sure. You know I called the sheriff."

"But you didn't. We were talking . . ."

"But I did after that. It was while you were putting the moon rock in the try net, I guess."

"Gee, thanks for telling me. You could have saved me a whole bunch of worry, you know."

"When did I have time?"

"I don't know. We did all right, I guess." Joseph stood up and waved to the helicopter.

"Are you boys all right?" a voice asked through a megaphone. Joseph could have bet that the voice belonged to Vince Pierce.

Joseph and Huy both waved and shouted, "Yes!"

"Okay," the voice said, "the coast guard is on its way."

Pete struggled to a sitting position and stared at them.

"Can't you at least get some of these stinking crabs off of me?" he asked.

"Can't you at least say, 'please'?" Joseph asked.

"So, *please*. All right?"

"I guess. I'll get a broom." He looked at Huy. "Your mother will have a fit when she sees the mess this boat is in."

Huy looked around, nodding silently.

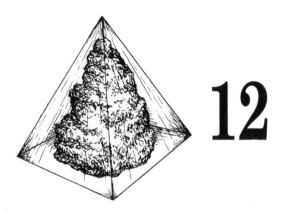

12

Joseph was glad that the crying was over. His mother had cried; Mrs. Ta had cried; and he had struggled with the possibility when a great lump had risen in his throat. But now, moving along at top speed toward Galveston to join the other shrimpers which were to be blessed by the priest, everyone was far too busy cleaning and repairing the damaged decorations to think of crying.

Joseph's mother had cried first when, escorted by the coast guard, they had come in at the dock. There, in front of everyone, she hugged him and cried. The number of people who had gathered to meet them amazed Joseph. His mother, the Tas, city police, federal investigators, and even a few news reporters were standing on the wharf to greet them and ask questions.

His mother wept a second time when Joseph confessed his part in the recovery of the moon rock and then showed her his infected leg.

Joseph could not be sure whether Mrs. Ta's tears were from relief for Huy's safety or from dismay over the condition of the boat, but she shed enough of them to cover both cases.

Vince Pierce had been great. He had lowered himself from the helicopter onto the shrimper and had taken charge of Pete. He freed Pete from the net, handcuffed him, and before they reached the shore, had gotten a partial confession. He had also rescued Lonesome from the hold by picking him up and carrying him up the ladder to the deck. There Lonesome stood guard in front of Pete, snarling occasionally when Pete moved.

At the dock, Vince had taken charge in a quiet, professional manner. After turning the moon rock and Pete over to his federal colleagues, he answered the reporters' questions briefly and somehow managed to keep them away from the boys and their families during the first minutes of reunion. He gave them time to compose themselves before they had to submit to the inevitable, ridiculous questions that reporters sometimes ask in times of crisis.

"How do you feel?"

"Were you frightened?"

"Are you glad to see your son back safe and sound?"

Joseph's mother fielded that one neatly. "No," she answered, smiling sweetly at the reporter, "I was hoping he would be maimed for life for slipping out and not telling me where he was going."

Mrs. Ta, who understood very little of what was said, simply cried again.

When the crowd thinned, Mr. Ta insisted that they prepare to leave for Galveston. No matter how the boat looked, he was determined that it should be blessed before he began a season of dangerous shrimping in the gulf. He guided his own family on board. Joseph and his mother followed. Vince spoke hastily to the officers and ran to get on board just as the engine started.

Now Joseph leaned over the side, rinsing the mud from the try net by letting it drag across the top of the water as they made their way toward Galveston. His mother stood near him, brushing away mud and fluffing

99

the bright-colored whiskers of the main net so that they would blow gracefully as the breeze caught them.

"Mother," Joseph asked, pulling the net over the side and hoisting it to its proper place, "how come you were at the dock?"

"Mother's instinct," she answered simply.

"No, really," Joseph insisted, "how did you know?"

"Mother's instinct," she repeated. "I woke up feeling uneasy; you weren't there; you had left no note; you had not told me you were going out early this morning; and I just knew that something was wrong. I went first to the Ta boat and when I saw it was gone, I went to the police station. I caught Mr. Pierce just leaving to go to the helicopter. Huy's call had already come in."

"Oh," Joseph looked at her guiltily. "I'm sorry. I guess there is something to this mother's instinct, huh?"

"There is, and there is also something to this mother's wrath. If you ever do anything like this again, I will maim you for life myself." Tears filled her eyes again. She stopped her work and came over to hug him.

"I'm sorry," he said against her shoulder. "I really am. I know that I should have told you and Vince as soon as we found the rock."

"Right!" she said, letting him go and turning back to her whiskers. "And, if there is a next time, you will. Right?"

"Yeah." Joseph hesitated. "You know, Mom, there might be a next time. I like Vince. I might like to be a federal investigator when I get out of school."

"You might?" She glanced at him, smiled, then gave the net a final shake. "Well, at least we have a few more years to talk about it."

Having finished their task, they looked around to see what still needed to be done.

Vince had attacked the job of cleaning both Huy and the floor of the deck in the same manner. He hauled up bay water in a bucket tied to a rope and poured it over Huy. During the process, Huy had taken the cold water stoically; but, afterward, he rubbed himself vigorously with a towel and danced from one foot to the other in order to warm up. Now, still slightly damp but clean, he was sweeping the water that Vince poured on the deck over the side.

Mrs. Ta was working with a string of rather droopy flowers which had fallen from the rail at the back of the deck. Lonesome lay in his coiled rope, watching everyone and shaking his head occasionally when a spray of water caught him.

"Ahoy, avast, and all those sailor-sounding things," said Vince, putting his hand on the small of his back and straightening up. "What do you think, Huy? Is that about the best we can do?" Vince had rolled up his jeans, but his shoes were soaked and made a squishy sound when he walked.

Mrs. Ta turned to look at the wet deck. "For now," she answered for Huy, "it will do."

Vince smiled at her and came to stand beside Joseph and his mother. "Are you two okay now?" he asked.

"Sure." Joseph's mother put her hand on Vince's arm and looked up at him. "Thanks for all you have done."

"Don't mention it. The problem now is, what are we going to do with this foolhardy, independent, detective son of yours?" He turned to Joseph. "Why, Joseph? Why did you try to do it alone? Was it to protect your mother? The Tas? Jan?"

Joseph nodded his head. "All of that, I guess. I thought that you just wanted the rock back. That's what Dr. Wilhelm said in assembly."

"But this is much bigger than that, Joseph. This is international theft."

"But I didn't know."

"I know you didn't, but that is just another reason you should always go to the authorities when you have information about a crime. They may have a bigger picture of it than you do. We have known since last Friday that this was not a simple schoolboy prank."

101

"How?"

"The yacht of a very wealthy South American art collector anchored in the gulf a few miles out from Roll Over Pass that day. His yachts have been conveniently near several art thefts in the past few years. We were hoping to get some hard evidence against him this time."

"Did I ruin it?"

"Maybe not. Pete was to meet Señor Martinez's men this morning. One of our investigators will take his place. You may have even made it easier for us."

"Gee, I hope so."

"So do I. But let me tell you, young man, you and Huy had me worried."

"Why?"

"Your change in attitude toward me after Friday. You avoided me and were no longer as friendly and open as you were at first. I actually suspected for a while that you knew what was taking place and that you had been sucked into the deal by Pete and Mr. Kelly."

"Mr. Kelly?"

"Yes. We have been watching him too. He has also been conveniently near the same art thefts that Señor Martinez has."

"And Pete?"

"Just working for Kelly. I thought he spent his nights on the bluff waiting for a signal from Señor Martinez. Now I know he was just watching for you and Huy. By the way, tell me something. How did you find where the rock was hidden?"

"It was Lonesome. You remember how he barked that afternoon when we were down by Meeks pier? We went back after you left, and he did the same thing again. He was after a scrap of Huy's coat. We followed him out there, but Pete saw us afterwards and threatened to hurt Mom and burn Mr. Ta's boat if he ever saw us around there again."

"So that was when you decided to take over alone?"

"I guess so."

Mrs. Ta turned from her work and came toward them. "Huy's coat? Did I hear you say you found Huy's coat?"

"Yes, ma'am."

"Where is it?"

Joseph dropped his head. "I left it in the culvert at school," he answered.

"Oh, dear!" She shook her head sadly. "It will be ruined, but I shall tell Mr. Ta. He has been so concerned about it." She started toward the pilot house. Huy and Joseph exchanged glances and grinned.

Joseph had put off asking his last question as long as he could. He took a deep breath. "What will happen to Pete and . . ." He stopped.

"And Jan." Vince finished for him. "I don't know. I can tell you that Jan came to us this morning at the police station and told us that she suspected that you were in danger. It seems that Pete had phoned her when he discovered that the rock was missing, and she knew that he thought you and Huy got it. She came directly to the police and filled us in on everything that she knew."

"She did?"

"Yes. That is how we know that Pete was supposed to meet the man at Roll Over Pass this morning. She was very helpful. It may help in her defense at the trial."

Joseph turned away and gazed out over the water. Pictures of Jan, fast and strong on the tennis court, smiling and friendly in the halls, carefree and windblown on the beach, came to his mind. He knew the images would stay with him a long time.

A long blast of the shrimper's horn brought Joseph out of his reverie.

"Fleet dead ahead!" Mr. Ta shouted from the pilot house.

Gaily decorated shrimpers were slowly making their way down an alley left by the many boats anchored in the gulf. The crowd of spectators in the boats clapped and cheered each shrimper as it made its way to the platform where the priest waited.

Huy's younger sisters scampered down from the pilot house, where their mother had insisted they stay until the boat was cleaned up. They scooted along the narrow passageway at the side of the pilot house in order to lean across the front rail. Mrs. Ta hurried after them and stood protectively close by.

Huy threw up his arms in a sign of victory. "We are going to make it," he shouted. "We'll be last, but at least we'll make it."

"I hoped we would," Mrs. Boyd said. "Mr. Ta would have been so bitterly disappointed."

When Mr. Ta maneuvered his boat into the alley, there was a swell of applause and shouting. At first, Joseph assumed that this was the normal greeting for each of the shrimpers as they passed, but it soon became evident that they were being singled out for special attention. He began to recognize faces and voices.

"Hey, Joseph . . . hey, Huy . . . way to go!"

"What do you know? Kelly's Landing has its own Hardy Boys!"

Joseph waved but was too astonished to return the greetings. "How do they know about us?" he asked.

"Ship-to-shore radio and the police wavelength are very easy to monitor." Vince shrugged. "Your fame has been spreading all morning, I guess." His face suddenly brightened and he waved toward the dock. "Now there is a mighty pretty lady whom I called and told about it myself," he said.

Miss Duncan did look "mighty pretty" with the wind whipping her full, pale-blue skirt around her and the sun lighting her long, auburn hair. Standing rather unsteadily atop an old oil drum, she leaned forward, clinging with one hand to a light pole and waving excitedly with the other.

"You are not getting rid of me entirely, you know,"

Vince continued, winking at Joseph. "I'm going to be spending most of my free time right here."

"Gee, that's great," Joseph said.

"Yes," Huy's dark eyes sparkled, "perhaps we can get some more volunteer work from you in the library."

"That is very likely," Vince agreed.

Jack Washington, towering above everyone else on the dock, cupped his hands to his mouth and yelled.

"Hey, Pierce," he called. "I made it. They interviewed me on TV. I'm a star!"

"That's true. That's true." Mr. Greyson was standing beside Jack. "He did very well, very well indeed."

They approached the place where the white-robed priest stood on a high platform. He lifted his arm. Drops of holy water fell across the bow. The crowd fell silent.

"Our God," Father Schmidt began, "we invoke your blessing on the captain and the laborers of this vessel. We ask that you grant them good weather, safe passage, and abundant harvest. Our God, we thank you for your generous mercy and your protection of Joseph Boyd and Huy Ta . . ."

Joseph had never received a blessing from a priest before. He did not hear the last lines of the father's benediction. Somehow, his eyes kept misting over, and he didn't want anyone on board nor the TV cameras to see them.

Lonesome nudged Joseph's leg as if he understood. Joseph knelt and hugged him. A few tears trickled unnoticed into Lonesome's soft, black coat.